A Killing in Samana

A Chris Allard Mystery

by Richard Schwindt

Don't feel guilty about vacationing. What are you truly living and working for anyways? Death is all too real.

Richie Norton

Demonic spirits never sleep or take a vacation, always plotting and waiting for the next offensive.

E.A. Bucchianeri

"It's a fucking bomb," Tony said.

"No shit, Sherlock," Marie said from her knees, "And it's set to go off in ten minutes."

"Christ, Marie, get rid of it!" Courtney said.

"Nope, we'll just set it off; I think it's C4; no we have to get rid of the passengers." Our shock must have shown but she had turned to face the stern and everyone on board.

"ATTENTION!" My name is Lieutenant Commander Marie Lesage of the Royal Canadian Navy and I am taking command of this vessel. Now hear this, do every fucking thing I say and you might live."

She had our attention.

Table of Contents

Introduction

Although they hail from Scarborough, Ontario and inhabit the same timeline; it was never clear whether Chris Allard, Tony Price and Courtney Snow lived in the same universe. After all, Tony and Courtney's universe contained distinct paranormal phenomenon; Chris's did not.

It turns out that not only do they occupy the same reality but their lives are about to converge; and not in Scarborough.

It would be fun and helpful to read the various prequels – *The Death in Sioux Lookout trilogy, Tony Price: Confidential, Herkimer's Nose* – but it's not necessary. *A Killing in Samana* is a stand-alone novel.

Chris Allard is the default narrator, but my readers know I like to mix things up and let other characters tell some of the story, especially his always skeptical wife, Kate.

As denizens of an affluent and cold country, Canadians are often privileged to be temporary guests in warm weather destinations during the winter months.

The country I have visited the most, furnishing the setting for this story, is the Dominican Republic. As noted in the book, Samana, on the northeastern coast of the DR, has a fascinating and unique history.

Sunbeams International Resorts is a fictional company.

July1830, Hispaniola, the north coast

Lucy Jones, 23, had arrived a week earlier by steamer from Philadelphia. It seemed to her that she had travelled forever from the cotton fields of Georgia. She missed the United States; not the slavery, never the slavery, but this place felt foreign and hot, so hot.

Hilly and wild, the north coast of Hispaniola twisted with palms, forest and cut over brush.

She spoke English, and they spoke Spanish, Creole, French; it didn't matter; it was all incomprehensible. Her people were sometimes welcomed but not always trusted.

After Lucy's mother picked up a fever on the boat she feared for her health. They didn't have money; so she would need to approach people in the church community for help. But she so wanted to be independent.

Thus, when Captain Reed offered to pay her for a days' work she accepted.

On that windy night prior, mother took a turn for the worse, her fever spiked and then... she took her last breath. Two nice ladies from the church came to help but Lucy sat by the door on their single stool, too stunned to speak or even cry.

When Reed appeared the next morning, she walked out the door, leaving the remains covered with a thin blanket.

They set out into the bay in his small dinghy. The water was rough; he rowed hard. She shivered in the bow; wondering where he planned to take her and what the work would entail.

The chop finally threw them into the ochre sand of a small beach, under hill and palm, isolated from nearby villages. They disembarked.

Lucy was not naïve, but she didn't expect what came next as he grabbed her and tore at her clothes. But he was still catching his breath from the rowing; she broke away and ran into the sea.

"Come back here, you stupid cow," he shouted.

She felt only despair. There was no need to fight. The water; cool and lovely, carried her forward until an undertow delivered her into Poseidon's final embrace.

November, 2018, Thursday morning at Samana airport, Dominican Republic

I savour those first moments; the walk from the plane on the tarmac to the barren confines of a small airport, the tender mercies of customs officers and local vendors, waves of humid air, palm fronds blown madly by trade winds at the runway's fringe.

Kate disappeared into the ladies' room so I made it through the formalities first. Luggage in tow, I stepped out the door into the hot morning air. We had often vacationed in the Dominican Republic, though this was our first visit to Samana on the northeast coast.

Exposed to the full effects of the sun, capping my eyes with a hand, I looked up into the expansive sky and scattered clouds fading into eternity. Unseen birds shrieked from the trees.

I looked around for the bus to the resort. It was parked right in front of my nose, but Kate hadn't appeared.

You dress as lightly as you can fleeing the Canadian winter, but making your way from home to the airport at 4 am on a frigid morning you can't get away with much. You still arrive in the tropics overdressed. The Dockers and cerise golf shirt stuck to my skin.

I handed over luggage and two US bills to the attendant and climbed on board. One of the first, I took a seat at the front so I could catch the scenery on our way to resort. Grubbing through my knapsack, I pulled out a cream golf cap and a pair of sunglasses.

Laying back in the seat, I took a moment to measure what ached or creaked. These trips felt more like work every year and I had turned 66 on my last birthday. Taking on the lineups and expansive madness of Pearson Airport in the wee hours seemed a young mans' game.

But social workers rarely retire wealthy so Kate and I bargain hunted trips and found the best we could with the funds we had.

The self-pity dissipated. We were off to an all-inclusive holiday at the five star Sunbeams International resort where the staff bused in for 10 days at a stretch, away from their families, serving people like me for low wages.

My job was to have fun, be a good guest and tip well.

"Stop introspecting you dumb son of a bitch! You're on a fucking vacation!"

Did I mention we were not travelling alone? I had held the seat for my wife but it was now being occupied by Mister Tony Price.

"I saved that for Kate."

"Relax Chris, she and Brenda are chattering away and looking at sun hats. I brought something for you."

Tony threw a cane in front of him, opened his knapsack and started rummaging around.

A big guy; he had at least 5 inches on me, and broad shouldered. His hooded blue eyes had dimmed over the years and the always long black hair turned grey, but for a hard living guy he looked good.

"If they miss this bus…"

"You are such a goddam worrywart." He kept poking. "Ah, here."

Tony extracted a white plastic bag from his pack and from it, two sweating green cans of Presidente lager, and a small bottle of Barcelo rum.

"The luggage guy said that we have to stop at two other resorts before we hit ours and it will take at least an hour and a half."

"God forbid we should do that sober."

"Exactly!"

"Where did you find the booze?"

He grinned. Tony could find alcohol anywhere. I accepted the beer. We cracked the cans and took a deep swig. The rum followed, passed hand to hand. I coughed. He'd bought the cheap stuff.

"Thanks." He nodded, pleased with himself. I needed to stop being an ass. "How's your leg?" He shrugged and took another swig of the rum.

"This'll help."

Like me, Tony was a social worker. Three years earlier, in an alley of the Silver Birch Housing Project, one of his clients – armed, and wired on meth – shot him in the leg after Tony spirited the man's wife and son to safety.

By way of thanks for saving his family the man complained that Tony had sworn at him. His boss had taken the complaint, seized the opportunity to fire her most annoying employee, and sent Tony permanently to the sidelines.

He and his wife Brenda – another social worker – then moved from Scarborough to Kingston, following their twins who were completing degrees at Queens University.

Tony finished his beer, burped and reached into his pack for another.

"I haven't checked," I said, "Is there a washroom on the bus? I may have to take a leak before we get there."

"I don't know. Maybe you should have brought a diaper."

"Hilarious. How many of those beers did you buy?"

"You want another?"

"Yeah."

Tony and I were both social workers from Scarborough, raised as only sons of a single mother.

And that was where the similarity ended.

The other passengers were boarding and the driver and attendant shooing them in. We sat back to watch our fellow vacationers arrive.

Everyone looked worse for wear after the morning flight. Some had been up all night drinking. Others spent the previous evening running around, dropping off kids and dogs, working overtime and packing before a short sleep.

Collars stuck up, hand luggage flapped about awkwardly. A few people looked at our beers; the thought bubble reading: *"Where did they get those?"* Tony smiled serenely.

For all that, most folks relaxed and chatted. A few argued.

Some brought dazed looking children; some traveled with friends and others with partners.

An elbow dug into my ribs.

"What!"

A single man entered and fell. I briefly felt him sitting on my lap, facing away. Tall and skinny – drunk – he twisted, then turned away. His face was red, wrinkled and hidden by a mane of white hair and Santa Claus caliber beard.

Between us, we removed him from me so he could continue his precarious journey down the aisle.

"Poor bastards' alone and worse for wear," I commented.

"Don't be such a social worker, Chris. He'll drink his way through the week and be as happy as he is anywhere else."

"I'm mostly retired."

"Once a social worker, always a social worker."

"Nobody told us that in graduate school." He handed me the rum bottle.

The next sound came from a familiar source. "Chris, you didn't save me a seat?" This was my wife, Kate. I looked up.

"Tony took your seat."

She laughed.

"And you're into the beer."

"Tony brought it…" I wasn't going anywhere with this line. Another laugh followed

"Of course he did. Tony could find cold beer and vodka in the Sahara desert. You boys survive the trip?"

This would be Tony's wife, Brenda. We had been friends for years but I could never hear her voice without a twinge of guilt. Brenda was the best of women; warm, kind, smart and capable.

"I'm good, Brenda."

"Did you bring your blue pills, Chris?" Kate exclaimed. A few giggles emanated from the seats close by.

"I think they're packed with the quart of lube, grandma." More giggles.

My wife was a complex creature; the only one of the foursome not in social work. She was funny, caustic and dedicated to keeping me humble. Life had taken care of any issues I had with grandiosity, but old habits die hard.

Kate was articulate but shy; these days' people labelled it social anxiety. But once she got off the plane, far from home and responsibility, it cured her. I pretended to be shocked, but I found her hilarious when disinhibited.

Add a few drinks to the equation and she would be a blast.

"You two are embarrassing me," Tony said. More laughs. Nothing in this earthly realm would ever embarrass him.

"I see two seats at the back," Brenda said before grabbing Kate's arm and giving it a yank.

"Ola Amigos!" A handsome young man with a Che Guevara beard entered the bus, found a perch beside the driver then spoke to him in the distinctive rat-a-tat Dominican Spanish.

The bus broke inertia, backed out of its spot, turned and carried us out of the airport and into the countryside.

The route to the resorts followed a single two lane highway along the south flank of the peninsula, through countryside, hill country, ocean vistas, small villages and the town of Santa Bárbara de Samaná itself.

After a moment of monkeying around with the microphone, Edwin introduced himself and welcomed us to the country, told a few lame jokes and offered safety tips.

He noted that those of us going to Sunbeams International could expect to be onboard for more than an hour and might as well enjoy the ride.

He then regaled us with a brief history of the diaspora of former slaves who still lived in the northeastern corner of the island. The Haitian government had welcomed them during the 1820s; men and women who had been freed, or escaped and travelled north.

Many came to Hispaniola by steamer from Philadelphia, arriving with antebellum English, unique customs and the protestant religion. Much of this remarkable background remained intact today in the form of a small but resilient community scattered throughout Samana.

I watched the passing road as he spoke, where life formed and moved with the highway. Small cinderblock and frame houses painted in pastels had been constructed alongside, including businesses for exchanging money, grabbing a bite or buying a beer. Men, women, children conducted their finances, socialized and met up with family.

The old and new coexisted; contrasting the poor with a growing middle class. The bus competed with expensive cars, trucks filled with coconuts and building supplies, small scooters with bare-headed fearless young drivers, and the occasional dog.

I guessed that Tony and I were thinking the same thing, observing this through a social workers' filter. How many stories, unspoken truths and hidden aspirations could be found among these people who would form only the vaguest of fleeting memories?

Tony spoke, breaking my reverie.

"I think we should make a bet about which one of us gets laid first."

Glancing around, I tried to locate our wives.

"If they heard that, we'll both lose the bet." As soon as I turned back front someone began to sing.

Whiskey!
Whiskey makes you frisky!
Drink lots of whiskey!
Drink some whiskey every day day
Day day day daaaaaay…

I groaned. "There's always somebody on one of these buses making Canadians look like drunken baboons."

"The truth will out."

"I think it was that skinny white haired dude with the beard."

"Chris, this is a fucking vacation. Turn that brain off."

Our ride continued, through the town of Samana and beyond. We started to make stops and unload tired but hope-filled tourists.

Sunbeams Samana appeared on a rocky hillside, lined with trees and palms and white stairways descending to the ocean.

As soon as I realized how *vertical* this vacation would be I glanced at Tony, who continued to drink and gaze out the window.

His career, like mine many years earlier, evaporated in an instant. He had grown up, and later worked for thirty years in the Silver Birch housing project; a location that could only be called a shithole.

Following the shooting, he had been depressed – even left Scarborough, though he hid the loss of his raison d'être whenever we visited. I hoped he had found purpose again.

But even though he had been shoved aside by his workplace and profession, he had done it saving a woman and child from trauma, and possible death.

My career ended when I slept with a client. She had later been murdered while trying to find and forgive me. I worked as a consultant in Sioux Lookout, and a therapist to affluent people since, but it was no career.

"Chris, they're unloading the bags! Get off the bus and grab them." I needed to get out of my head; Kate glared at me from the aisle.

Later, in the room

I met Kate, and dumped Brenda, shortly after starting graduate school at the University of Toronto. In the long run; it was for the best. Brenda and Tony worked together in mysterious ways; and by being an asshole, I opened the gate to that relationship.

Kate could still turn heads, but she was a knockout back in the day. Lean, leggy and raven haired, she committed herself to her corporate consulting, me and our two daughters.

The esthetic of Dominican resorts, with their graceful lines, open plans and cool greens, yellows and pinks always appealed to me. The Iberian architecture with its Moorish roots worked well in tropical settings.

I looked around the room and out the window past the balcony as a cooling breeze wafted in from the ocean, Kate was checking out the bed. The room was perfect but she could never escape the idea that tropical rooms were damp.

"You found us a good room this time, Chris."

"Why thanks." I appreciated the acknowledgement, despite the implication that I usually didn't find good rooms.

"I know about your bet with Tony."

"Kate, my God, that was all Tony. I told him to shut up."

"People were joking about Grandpa and Grandma horny up and down the bus."

I groaned. "You had to mention blue pills."

"Relax Chris." Why did everyone keep telling me to relax? "Do you want to win that bet or not?"

"Oh." I turned towards the bed.

Confessions from the realm of social work

My taste in wine had followed a downward arc for years; as I cheapened and coarsened with age, so did the liquid in the glass at dinnertime. Now, even Dominican buffet wine did the job.

The four of us sat on the deck, taking sips of the pink stuff and discussing the day as the sun sank into the ocean, shedding riots of gamboge, and burnt orange light.

An artless wink on first meeting from Tony implied we may have to settle for a tie in our competition but I was eager to change the channel.

"How's your room?" I asked Brenda.

"Beautiful," she said. "I love the view. What's for dinner?"

"I guess we have to go check; I saw a sign saying something about Italian night."

"Pasta!"

After loading our plates the ruthless pull of our strange profession asserted itself. Or perhaps it was just therapy.

"If you could go back in a time machine, would you still choose social work?" I threw this out to the table. Kate seemed in an expansive mood and tolerant of our friends, so she let it slide.

"I don't think so," Tony started. "I worked in the Silver Birch housing project 30 years and, guess what, it's still there, still dysfunctional, people are stuck, and I'm walking around with a fucking limp."

"You got out," I said.

"Sure, a few people do; some in good ways like me – damn few – getting an education, but more via ambulance, police car or hearse. The place is fucked; a Trade college, public health team, or demolition crew could accomplish more than I did."

"That's not true, Tony," said his wife. "You burned out early – and it showed – but there was never a more pragmatic social worker on the planet. You did more small useful things for people…"

"That's the point, Brenda…" His voice had raised. A few people glanced over from other tables. Kate shivered as a rogue evening breeze wafted up from the sea.

"Sorry, hon," Tony continued following another slug of pink wine. "The things I did were little things; they just kept the damn social order in place. I'm glad I helped people; I am, but change anything; I don't think so."

"And now here I am drinking pink wine," he said, as if that was the worst of his sins.

"There's lots of rum in the room," Brenda said kindly. She had been watching Tony as he spoke.

She showed her age more than anyone; a career in Child Welfare could do that. The Brenda I had met in the 1970s was a stunning redhead, a loving and athletic woman, with a dry as dust sense of humour.

She was still a warm personality; highly organized and determined, but the white of her disarrayed hair now competed with thinning orange strands, and she was plump by any standard.

We all age, but there was something, including more wrinkles than the rest of us, which seemed to display her years.

It was tempting to attribute this to being married to a wild man like Tony but I believed he animated her. She would never have been happy with anyone else.

"And you, Brenda? Go back into social work?"

"In a heartbeat. It's who I am; or who I've become. It structures my compulsive need to help."

"I don't understand why you never burned out or turned into a bitch doing child protection in Scarborough all those years," Tony said, "abused kids, parents who threatened you, brain-fucked administrators; all the traumatic shit you faced."

"I don't know either," she said. "I think where you drank and swore Tony, I got depressed. Did you ever notice how many vacations I spent in bed?"

Anyone who didn't understand Brenda would have read anger, sarcasm or sexual innuendo into that comment. But her comment was devoid of nuance, a sincere question.

"Yes, I did. Then after a week or so you got up and went back to work." A moment of silence came to the table; we sat in the dimming light amidst the murmur from other tables.

"And you, Chris?" This was Brenda; only she had the decency to play it straight with me. I didn't look at Kate but she'd look at me.

"After I slept with Marianne in the 90s, the roof caved in; it appeared to destroy my world. It didn't, I still had Kate and the girls, but later, when she was murdered, I was close to suicidal. They stuck me in a bloody jail in Sioux Lookout until my father-in-law the lawyer got me out.

"But bourgeois fucking me found solace in treating rich and influential people. I still do it; and still enjoy it; working for Bob Wong; a guy I can call a friend."

"How bourgeois can someone from Scarborough be?" Tony asked.

"My mother was born to a wealthy family in the 16th arrondissement of Paris – you've met her Tony…"

"I'm still recovering."

"So you get it, we are the personification of bourgeois.

"So, ya, therapists never quit – mom was pushing ninety before she stopped – I survived a much deserved whipping and trip to the doghouse – and everything got better after that. I'd go back into social work."

Kate had sat silently through our disclosures, taking in everything. She knew better than most how self-obsessed social workers can become

"Can I say something?" she asked. It was her turn, and she didn't wait for an answer as eyes turned towards her.

"I don't think I've ever seen three people better at lying to themselves.

"It may surprise even Chris that I love social workers. But even the best I have met, possibly excluding Chris's buddies from Sioux Lookout, live with the fantasy that your profession matters."

It might have been false chivalry but Tony and I immediately glanced at Brenda. But she sat waiting to hear what Kate had to say.

"Your profession is made of air; it hardly has a knowledge base and even at the best of times run by pompous functionaries who would sell their mothers for a boost in funding. Tony, what did you call your bosses all those years; Fuckwad and Barfette?

"You help people. Everyone gets that but the goddam social workers themselves." Her eyes turned towards Brenda, "You rescued children from situations so horrible ordinary people would throw up if they understood.

"Tony, you got shot, but your being alive at all is a miracle. How many pimps and drug dealers trafficking to children did you stare down over the years? How many Fuckwads and Barfettes' did you have to get through to do the simplest thing to help your clients?

"For all I know you took out a few vampires and werewolves while you were at it."

Brenda shot a strange glance at Tony who looked away.

"And let me tell you about my husband," Kate continued. "His ego needs keeping in check, but Bob Wong has told me that Chris is the best natural therapist he's ever seen. He's never forgiven himself for Marianne; it was a dumb mistake, but *he* didn't murder her.

"As to being therapist to the rich; they are powerful and influence lots of people; someone has to do it, and no one does it better than the bourgeois social worker here."

"You are good smart people who did something wonderful with their lives. Not everyone gets that chance. Any of you who didn't go into social work again would be a fool."

Kate stopped on that note. We looked at her, speechless but grateful. It was so unlike her to speak out to a group unless she was working or, well, on vacation.

I had one more thing to say. "Why don't we take a walk on the beach?"

A surprise surrendered by the breaking waves

Tony acted like everything was alright when we made it to the bottom of the stairs.

"I'm too drunk to feel my leg," he said, convincing no one. We'd all seen him wince.

A brief tropical rainfall earlier had dampened the long white balustrade to sea level and we had all descended gingerly, holding onto the railing.

"Is this a stupid idea, Chris?" Like a contestant on Jeopardy, Kate liked to put statements in the form of a question.

"It's a beautiful evening; a short walk to the other end and then we can go listen to music by the pool."

As the last crimson slashes dimmed on the far horizon we walked feet in the water, sandals in hand. It was a wonderful feeling and the memories of a dismal Toronto November melted in the Caribbean night.

Despite the occasional puff of cool air the evening retained the day's residual warmth. Our senses were dominated by the sound of the waves breaking from the sea and the subtle sense of life around us.

A village could be found a kilometer past the end of the beach, which itself was a couple of hundred meters long.

At the foot of the stairs a whitewashed pier passed ragged stone walls, small crabs hid in crevices, and an artificial breakwater had been sunk to one side, ending with a whitewashed gazebo.

We agreed to do one circuit of the playa.

The absence of light plays on our sense of mystery. Tomorrow when we came to swim, read, drink beer and lay around this would be just another beach.

Tony had good eyes; he spotted a bundle bobbing in the waves first.

"Is that a log or a dead fish or something?" He pointed.

We all squinted to adjust to the fading light. A dark package of some kind seemed stuck on… oh shit, there was an arm.

Tony was first in the water, trying to wade in with his cane.

"Chris get in there and help him," Kate said sharply. I took one step before almost being toppled by a wave. "That person might be alive."

He wasn't far out. Tony and I were able to each grab an arm and use the force of the water to lift him the last few feet to shore.

One glance at the pathetic figure that Brenda and Kate helped us lay out confirmed no one would be doing CPR that night.

"We need some light," Brenda said.

"I've got a lighter," Tony said.

"You weren't going to smoke on this trip."

"I'm not, I still keep it around."

I activated the flashlight on my phone.

"You brought your phone?" Kate was always trying to separate me from that device. But at this moment, it came in handy.

We shuddered as a sad white bearded face, eyes closed in death, appeared in the sudden illumination. His long hair hung to one side dripping onto the sand.

"Poor bastard," Tony said, "that's the old drunk guy on the bus. He came down here too wasted to swim…" I looked closer.

"He looks familiar." Tony leaned in.

"Yeah, he does, I can't place him but I've seen him before."

Kate stood back, clutching her shirt under her throat with her right hand. She was starting to shiver, even though she hadn't gone in the water. Half looking down, she didn't hesitate. "That's Sergeant Miles, from the Sioux Lookout OPP."

Tony and I snapped right back to the corpse.

"Oh my God, it is Miles," I said.

"Fuck me, you're right, I can see it now," Tony said.

Brenda cleared her throat, head tilted, looking unbearably sad. She said: "Who is Sergeant Miles?"

Kate, on the aftermath

Brenda had run into the dark and up the stairs to fetch security, followed by local police and then, hours later, by two investigators from the Dominican National Police.

We had been speechless for a few moments, disturbed by the body at our feet, mentally reviewing our experiences with him. Though nothing to do with us, the discovery felt shameful, as if we should have done something to help the hurting alcoholic we had seen earlier.

"What's his first name?" Tony asked.

"I don't know, I just called him Miles or Sergeant Miles." The music had started by the pool; a manic merengue, probably accompanied by athletic dancers and a funny multi-lingual host.

Something clicked in my head. I looked at Tony. "Did you know him?"

"Yeah, I met him in Sioux Lookout."

"You went there for 2 weeks twenty-four years ago; how did you manage to meet the OPP Staff Sergeant?"

"It's a long story that ended with him telling me to get lost."

"Well, there's something else you and Chris have in common," I commented. "What happened to him? How did he end up like this?"

"He must have fallen in the water, or been too drunk to swim," Tony said.

"No, like this. You remember him; he looked like the Marlborough man, tall and handsome, not this poor skinny guy."

"Please step away from the body, lady and gentlemen."

Security had arrived, two serious looking men and one woman. They guided us to one side and asked us to wait for the police. The police, when they arrived, asked us some cursory questions, but they were waiting for someone else.

The death of a tourist at a resort would not be taken lightly. Huge swaths of the Dominican economy depended on visitors, and the perception of safety was paramount to the decision to go there or another Caribbean destination.

If it felt unsafe in the DR, a Canadian could simply decide to go to Cuba or the Mayan Riviera instead.

The wait seemed interminable; the night was warm but we were starting to shiver in the wind from the sea; Tony had to find a beach chair to take the burden off his leg.

By now a dozen Dominicans were standing by the corpse and guests milling at the top of the stairs, stopped from descending by nervous staff.

Brenda and Tony seemed unshaken but Chris was pacing around the sand. He may have solved three murders back in the day, but he was not a tough guy like Tony who could face down anyone or anything.

Two individuals in plain clothes, accompanied by others with a stretcher, joined the cluster by the shore, and began delivering crisp orders. Someone took pictures of the corpse. One of the police pointed to us.

The two people, figures in the dim light, turned towards us.

The first emerged into view as a tallish, handsome and strong looking man; looking closely at us with dark eyes and a serious expression. He was accompanied by an athletic short haired black woman.

Without preliminaries, he spoke. "I am Lieutenant Ortiz with the Dominican National Police and this is Private Panier who is assisting me." He pulled out a notebook and started to write.

"Êtes-vous Haïtien?" Chris said, looking at the Private. Before she could answer, the Lieutenant spoke:

"I believe we have one common language here, and will stick to that."

It had taken my husband mere seconds to piss him off. Chris nodded contritely.

"I will need your names, addresses and reasons why you were on the beach when you were."

After that was done, he noted: "The deceased individual was named Douglas Miles, single, from a place called…" He looked down at his book and frowned, "Sioux Lookout. He listed his occupation as retired."

"He was a senior police officer before he retired." Ortiz looked up sharply, then glanced over his shoulder at the group by the water. They were lifting Miles up by the shoulders, trying to transfer him to the stretcher. His clothes were waterlogged.

"You knew him?"

"I worked with him when I consulted in Sioux Lookout."

"I see." He again glanced down at the book. "You are listed as a retired social worker from Scarborough," He cocked his head to one side. "How would you work with a police officer?"

My alarm spiked, but even as Ortiz looked at Chris, Private Panier watched me. They had done some homework before this interview; these two were sharp and would brook no nonsense.

Chris would need to bite that smart tongue of his and under no circumstances go too far into exactly how he knew Miles.

"Some people were murdered while I was there. I helped him a little on the cases."

Now I wanted to murder Chris. Ortiz tapped his pen on the metal rings of the book but it was Panier who spoke:

"How exactly does a social worker from Scarborough get involved in a murder in Sioux Lookout?"

"I was in the wrong place at the wrong time."

"Just like tonight," she observed. Chris stood silently but couldn't have looked guiltier if he tried. Ortiz turned to me.

"And you Mrs. Michalchuk… you have a different name than your husband?"

"Yes."

"I see you are listed a business consultant."

"Yes."

"And you were also involved in murders in Sioux Lookout?"

"No."

Tony chuckled from his beach chair and Panier glanced back. His turn came next. Chris was the only person in the world that knew – or would ever know - I had committed one of the murders.

I wanted to make one point clear: "Miles looked different then. We didn't even recognize him until we saw him on the beach tonight." Ortiz nodded.

"The staff said that he was staggering around drunk since he arrived; not harming anyone but singing and acting the fool."

"That's what we saw."

A young man – more a boy - arrived with a tray with some large glasses of liquor. He was headed towards Tony, but Ortiz stopped him.

"*Que es eso?*" The young man looked like he wanted to flee.

"*El Senor Price llamó al servicio de habitaciones y pidió bebidas.*" After a glance at Tony, the officers turned their glare back to the hapless waiter.

"*Llévatelo, tonto, hasta que las entrevistas estén completes.*" The boy turned tail and left as quickly as he could with the tray. Tony would have to wait for his rum.

When Ortiz turned back to us, he ran his hands through his hair. "You are here for the week?" He asked but I had a feeling he already knew the answer. Chris nodded.

"We may need to speak to you again," Panier added. She looked again at me. What did she see?

"Just one more thing," Ortiz wasn't finished. "The body of your friend is going to the forensic laboratory in Santiago. But given his state of mind, this has the appearance of an unfortunate accident under the influence of alcohol."

"You don't suspect foul play?" Chris asked. I would have words with him later. But Ortiz took this surprisingly well. He sighed.

"A security guard is located at the far end of the beach. He saw nothing. It is unlikely that anyone could pass him. The staff saw Mr. Miles go down to the beach earlier but only you and your friends after that.

"People come to this country; they drink too much; sometimes take foolish risks. We find what appears to be a drowned man in the surf, we believe it is likely an accident. We will await the results of the autopsy but I have little doubt that it will be ruled death by accidental causes. You are free to go."

Chris opened his mouth to talk again but Ortiz cut him off.

"Thank you for drawing this incident to our attention but… we do not need a social worker from…" He paused, as if searching his memory. "…Scarborough, involved in this investigation."

Kate, the morning after

"Chris, come on, we'll be late for breakfast." He stood on the balcony, watching the approaching storm clouds and the verdant island across the restless water of the bay.

I had only slept a few hours; I am not sure he slept at all. He cried when we finally returned to the room; something new to him. He claimed it was common in old men and old therapists.

We had not returned to the room until 3 am. I had wanted to chew Chris out for stupid comments made, but didn't have the heart.

And the part of me that was beyond exhausted from a long and emotional day wanted to laugh hysterically at how Miles might be dead but his spirit lived on in Lieutenant Ortiz.

A late breakfast

The morning staff mounted snow white drapes across the deck in anticipation of rain, while scarlet and green Croton leaves waved in the escalating wind from stone-walled gardens.

We were ushered to a table for four; already occupied, by Molly and Steve from Orillia.

Tony and Brenda hadn't yet made it down.

Meeting up with others was the last thing I wanted, but I needed breakfast. I knew Kate would hate this but she put on a brave smile during the introductions then fled for the buffet.

As we settled in with our coffee and ham omelettes we learned about Steve and Molly's careers in municipal waterworks, and how Aruba had been too expensive this year so they had to settle for Samana.

Molly, decked out in a flowered sun dress, large straw hat and fly-goggle shades, appeared a travelling Diva, but some people do on vacation. Steve smiled and nodded on cue. He was a big guy; muscular too, a 'roid head?

"Oh my God," she said dramatically in a high pitched voice. "If it rains all the evidence will be destroyed!"

"Evidence of what?" I asked. Kate coughed up a piece of fruit; I wasn't sure if it was for real or to distract, but Molly continued:

"Some people found a dead body on the beach last night!"

"Wow. What happened?"

"No one seems to know. Someone at the bar told Steve that a group of social workers found it. By the way, what do you do?"

"I'm retired," I said quickly. "Kate was a business consultant."

"I see," she said. "Well, this is terrible. You probably shouldn't leave the property here." Kate gave me a poke underneath the table. "You don't know who is going to be out there in the dark."

"The beach here is property," I pointed out.

"We're going to the cigar factory today," Steve said. Maybe he found Molly grating too.

"Well, have fun; we have to meet some friends. Honey, you ready?" Kate nodded.

We were climbing the balustrade from the deck to the pool shortly after.

"I hope we don't have to hear about the death all week," she said.

"I doubt it. People are going to quickly revert to dopey hedonism under the sun and the eyes of tired bemused staff who have seen it all." I hoped I was right.

The sun appeared to be in retreat and the weather looked foreboding. Layered slate coloured clouds advanced, like an army surrounding the enemy before striking.

"We should check in with Tony and Brenda. I had no idea he met Miles. And Brenda - how does she feel? A corpse turns up on the beach and she's the only one who doesn't know him."

"Kate." I touched her shoulder and she stopped and turned on the stairway. "The woman said evidence. You don't think it was murder, do you?"

"Shut up, Chris! Really, don't talk like that. You always think bodies are murdered when you find them."

"And I'm always right."

"This is not one of those times. And it's none of your business. We're in a foreign country and *their* police are on it."

"Why was Miles here looking like he was a hundred years old, and why was he drunk? How does a former police officer end up dead on a Dominican beach?"

"I don't know and I don't care, Chris. But use your head; you would be the first to say policing is a stressful occupation. I don't know what happened to Miles – I always liked him – but the story is over now."

Rain began to fall.

The bar on the balcony

They were waiting for us, sitting across from each other, drinking beer. Tony looked serene but his tapping finger on the arm of his chair revealed the lack of sleep and tension. They had snagged a plum seat with a great view of the bay, out of the rain.

"Beer for breakfast?" Kate asked.

"We got some room service… I don't know whether you would call it early or late," he said.

"You okay?" I was looking at Brenda.

"Just fine," she said. "How about you? I think you knew Miles the best, Chris." We seated ourselves, and spoke to a waiter to order drinks before I answered.

"I feel guilty. I have no idea why, but if you knew Miles in his prime he was a formidable, strong and straight up guy. He hated seeing me around any kind of murder, and even arrested me once, but he was always decent to me.

"To see him like that…" I decided to change the subject.

"What did you think of Ortiz?"

Tony answered: "He was okay. He reminded me of Miles."

"No buzz on the evil detector?"

"No more than anyone else. That assistant of his though; something different about her."

Tony had grown up in an impoverished neighborhood, raised by a mom who was sick with cancer from the time he was a young teenager until she died, just before he began graduate school.

His rough edges were obvious; he swore like a sailor, drank heavily and displayed some weird quirks.

Tony claimed he could tell the percentage of good and evil in anyone; I don't know if anyone believed him, but he had certainly seen enough bad folks in his lifetime. After growing up in the Silver Birch housing project he returned after graduation and worked there for thirty years.

Even stranger, every now and again he would talk about monsters he'd seen and fought.

As if reading my thoughts, he added to his statement: "I don't think she's a werewolf."

"Oh good God, Tony, not that again. That was probably just a big dog."

Many years before, he, Brenda and I had an encounter with a large canine in the tunnels underneath Carleton University. He always claimed it was a werewolf.

"And how do you explain it talking to me?"

"Probably just some strange bark or growl." I looked to Brenda for support but she just shrugged, likely resigned to her husband's eccentricities. One thing I could intuit was my wife getting progressively more pissed off. So, I again changed the subject.

"So how *did* you know Miles?" The beer had arrived and I took the opportunity for a deep drink.

"That was the time a possessed Sasquatch kidnapped an American hunter. Colin Kowlchuk, Gilbert Armstrong and I became involved."

"Fine, be like that." I wanted to sound angry but I was used to this nonsense from him and had, to my surprise, steadily become fonder of Tony over the years. In the end, he was a good man and both of us – raised without fathers – appreciated good men.

"Miles didn't want a goddam social worker from Scarborough mixed up in a local case. Does that sound familiar?"

Kate chuckled. "If I had a buck for every time Miles said that to Chris, I could have retired early," she said. "Tony, what was different about Private Panier?"

We turned as a chill wind blew in from the sea. The first tentative drops of water evolved into a steady downpour. In the distance, we could just make out the recalcitrant sun, promising to rescue the day in about 20 minutes.

"I think this is light beer," Tony said.

"Private Panier?" Kate repeated.

"I think she might be like me, intuits evil. Handy for Ortiz to have around. Did you watch? They work well together, they can play each other's moves."

Brenda had been quietly observing this exchange.

"It's just an accident right?" She looked at me. Even in her mid-sixties, plump and aged she caused something in me to stir. And that had changed in the last few years. I couldn't put my finger on why, but she had somehow become sexier.

She had been a superlative runner in her youth, winning many track meets. This had been displaced over time by years of workaholic commitment to child welfare, and engagement with her wild-man boyfriend, then husband.

The arrival of twins, now in their early twenties, had stabilized the relationship.

"You still here, Chris?" Not much got by Kate.

"I don't know," I said. I pulled my thoughts away from Brenda. My beer had arrived and I took a swallow. "I think you are right, Tony, this tastes like light beer. Maybe, we're better off sticking to rum."

Kate glared at me. No one was providing a straight answer today.

"I find it strange," I said, "that it came to this. I suppose a drunk guy could drown in the surf, but it's not the Miles I knew."

"You didn't know him well as a person, Chris." Kate pointed out. I shrugged and drank some more beer.

"Yeah, you're right. It's a sad end to what looked like a sad guy." This ended the conversation but his death still felt wrong.

The rain tapered, then stopped as suddenly as it began. Time to go to the beach.

Wednesday morning

Ortiz and Panier appeared early. We were called in our rooms, and sent to a conference room just off of the lobby. Tony and Brenda arrived after us.

We enjoyed our week; ate and drank too much, avoided stomach distress and minimized sunburn. We were to depart the next day but had not forgotten the shadow of death.

The meeting didn't amount to much.

"We wish to thank you for your assistance," Ortiz began. "However, our Coroner has declared this an accidental death. Mr. Miles had excessive blood alcohol and appears to have fallen and struck his head, then subsequently drowned."

"Struck his head on what?" I had to ask. Private Panier shrugged.

"A blunt object in the water. Perhaps a rock or piece of wood. I do not think we will ever know."

"You don't think someone struck him with a piece of rock or wood?"

"Chris!" Kate hissed. But Ortiz responded.

"It does not seem like a plausible scenario. If you apply the principle of Occam's razor the obvious explanation is that a drunk man fell in the water and struck his head."

"How high was his blood alcohol count?"

"Not so much as you might think, but enough for intoxication."

Their body language suggested an end to the discussion. But Private Panier got the last word:

"On behalf of the Dominican government we want to express our regret for this sad event. We hope that this will not prevent you from returning at a future date."

And so it ended. We returned to the beach for our final day and evening of hedonistic withdrawal and left the morning after for Canada.

December, 2018, North Scarborough, preparing for an early Christmas dinner

"Chris, you need to leave in the next hour and pick up your mom before Roxie and Brett arrive."

"Can't Angela get her?"

"She called. She has a session that won't end until seven. She'll be here for dinner but your mom will want to be here earlier in the thick of things."

"Yes she will." I looked again out the window as we tried to put everything in place for Christmas.

Wet snow fell in sheets, like white rain. My long time neighbor Jimmy Li's son, Jon, had come by to try and clear his parent's driveway; head down, swearing under his breath. This snow was heavy. Traffic would slow and then constrict like a clogged artery.

Roxy had called from the Thunder Bay airport to say that their flight was expected to be on time. She had been scheduled to work over Christmas day so we were doing the celebration early.

She wanted to come. I had been back and forth from Sioux Lookout in winter enough times to know what a crappy trip it could be. I tried to talk her out of it but she said she had something to tell us and wanted her *grand 'mere* present.

They had been working on baby generation for a while now so it wasn't hard to guess what the announcement might be. We – future grandparents – were over the moon.

"The flight will be fine," Kate said before I could articulate my fear. "If they made it as far as Thunder Bay the rest is easy."

She was right; that's where the real plane would depart, but I would worry until she walked through the door.

Two weeks earlier...

I called Sioux Lookout as soon as we made it in the house from Samana.

"Ontario Provincial Police. How may I direct your call?"

"Detective Kosinski please."

"Just one moment, sir." I always got a kick out of surprising her at work.

"Detective Roxane Kosinski."

"Hey beautiful daughter. How's it shaking?"

"Dad! You're back! I was worried about you two. Everyone here is talking about Doug Miles. Are you and mom okay?"

"Tip top." And for the most part we were. I heard Kate yell from the bedroom, where she was unpacking, asking why I was bugging Roxy at work. I ignored her.

"What was up with him, Roxy?"

"Dad, I can't talk about this now but we'll be there soon."

Kate appeared from the bedroom. "Chris, you need to let this go." She followed this with a not so veiled threat. "I am going to be *really* pissed if you raise this at Christmas."

Christmas dinner

"So what if Miles was murdered?" I said

"Dad!" said my daughter, Roxy.

"Oh my God, Dad," said my other daughter, Angela.

"I talked to you about this, Chris," said my wife.

"Chrees, I need to know every'ting," said my 94 year old mother.

Only my son in law, Brett, kept his opinion to himself. He was on the OPP equivalent of a SWAT team. He had recently received a citation for leading a team to a cabin along a remote stretch of the Trans-Canada highway in Northwestern Ontario where they took down a gang of armed drug dealers.

He was brave, but not brave enough to take on the women in my family.

We dealt with the business about the baby with a champagne toast shared by everyone (life is weirdly unfair this way) but the expectant mother.

So we were in a good mood.

My mother remained in generally good health, aside from the common maladies of old age. She still got on with just a cane, though we lived in fear of a fall. She was slightly deaf, but maintained the razor sharp intellect that had earned her a wall full of degrees.

She had worked as a psychoanalyst until a great age, finally declaring she would rather being lying on her couch with a good book than sitting beside it listening to someone else's life.

The differing temperaments of my daughters had played out in their career choices. The younger, Roxy, had chosen policing as an outlet for her energy and martial temperament.

Angela upheld the family tradition and became a psychotherapist, though in a polite "I'm my own woman" choice she had completed a Ph.D. in psychology. Mom was initially appalled but relented when Angela swore she would never embrace behaviorism.

"I hate to say it, Dad; even assuming he was, we will never know. If the Dominican police don't think its murder, that's that. Unless you think that Ortiz guy was corrupt or something."

"No, I don't think so; he seemed pretty straight. Tony thought he was straight and he's never wrong about that sort of thing."

Kate raised her eyebrows and I looked back, trying to say that she had better not let *him* know I believed in his intuition.

I looked back to Roxy. She would never give me the satisfaction of saying, "Dad, only one of us is a real detective."

But I knew she was thinking it.

"Roxane," said my mother. "I had barely the acquaintance of thees Miles… tell us what you know."

Mom had met Miles for a few minutes during a vacation in Sioux Lookout. That was all she needed to assess someone. She wasn't psychic like Tony but processed information about human beings at lightning speed. I suspected that she was saving her insights to the last.

"Not much, *grand 'mere*. Doug Miles was considered a cop's cop. He belonged in Sioux. He liked hockey, fishing and hunting. Honest as the day was long; not a racist; he had a good arrest record, and part of the reason for that was the indigenous population trusted him."

"Family?" Angela leaned in. She wasn't going to be left out of any psychoanalyzing of poor Miles.

"He has a son in Thunder Bay – another cop; a lot like his dad; good guy, straight up. After Miles retired five years ago his wife died of cancer. They were close; good marriage; that's not easy for cops."

She unconsciously glanced at Brett, caught herself and rolled her eyes. In a room full of first rate therapists every gesture was noticed. He noticed too and decided to take another pull from his wine.

"He was fine after she died; well, not fine but you know, grieving the way anyone else does. Then about a year later he started to drink. I don't know if he was bored or lonely or what but he made a fool of himself, coming into the station loud and pissed. The guys were embarrassed for him. It was sad."

"What a letdown," I said. "That does not sound at all like the Miles I knew."

"You saw what he was like at the resort, Chris," Kate said. She didn't enjoy this conversation but knew better than to try stopping Allards in full flow. "It was pathetic."

"About a year later?" *Maman* had been listening intently. "And do not worry about the loving glance to your 'usband, Roxane; better to resume marital intimacy; you have not done so in about 2 weeks."

The table went silent. Roxy's eyes widened and Brett, spit up some wine then tried to look anywhere but at the people sitting around him. I am sure he had already decided that my mother was a witch.

"Marie-Giselle, we've talked about this." Kate would not stop Allard conversation mid flow but she would censor its excesses.

My mother didn't respond but assumed an innocent expression. But I knew from experience that she would respect Kates sanction.

I reached behind me for the other bottle of Bordeaux, open and breathing, on the counter top behind me, and placed it in front of Brett.

Angela laughed out loud and Roxy shot her sister a dirty glance. But she was not deterred.

"Grand'Mere, is there something significant about the year?" Mom put her hands in prayer formation in front of her mouth then removed them. She didn't speak for a moment as she formulated her thoughts.

"I believe this man would fall to peeces quickly as the stress finally breaks through the resistance. But I theenk not then; not this man." Mom seemed puzzled but I was waiting for something else.

"Grief is painful… but natural. The loss of the wife; it is tragedy but one we understand. He does not greeve normally for a year then suddenly let loose. And he does not make the display of himself in a public place; one long associated with work and responsibility. That would imply… a different man."

"Grand'Mere, we don't know what he had bottled up inside and when it would come out. Police carry a lot of stuff inside…" Angela joined the conversation.

I was fascinated by the sight of my mother and daughter arguing over psychology. They loved each other but were too much alike. I knew better than to put my two cents worth in.

"Angela, your grandma is right." Brett spoke. If he was annoyed at the Allard clan it didn't show. It was one of the reasons we all liked him. "Carter Miles was one of my best buds growing up. We played hockey together and hung out at each other's homes. So I saw his mom and dad together all the time.

"Doug was really bent out of shape when Marlene died. He cried, but in private. He hurt, got depressed and spoke to his closest friends. I think he even saw a therapist a few times."

"Of course he did, hon." Roxy put her hand on his arm. Tough as she was, it was easy for her to imagine losing a spouse who took the front row when violent criminals got loose.

"No, I'm saying he really grieved. It's not unusual for cops to see people grieving. We know what it looks like. He missed her desperately, but he went through all the emotions you would expect.

"So Marie-Giselle, you are right. There is something wrong about him suddenly falling to pieces. It didn't make sense then and it still doesn't but... I guess it doesn't matter now."

"Who wants cake?" I said. If this sounds flip; it was time to change the channel. This was supposed to be a celebration, not a lament for the dead, though I suppose it was a conversation we needed to have.

I had raised the subject, so maybe I should be the one to end it.

My mother was an empathetic woman; I often suspected it was the caring – not all the psychoanalytic mumbo jumbo – that made her such a successful Psychoanalyst.

I could see she understood how personal this loss would be for Brett even while secretly patting herself on the back for being right.

"Have you talked to Carter?" Kate asked. I stood up to fetch the alarmingly garish Croquembouche mom persuaded a baker friend to prepare for the occasion.

"We are going to go in and see him on our way back to Sioux," Brett said. This is going to be a difficult... Christ, what is that?"

"Croquembouche," Angela said, as if the identity of that most unctuous of French confections would be obvious to anyone.

She was smiling and loved her sister and her sister's hubby. But she didn't relish losing a psychology contest to her grandmother.

As I mentioned, they were a lot alike.

Later, Kate and I scrambled around for blankets, pillows and other necessities. Between the wine and the snow it made sense for everyone to stay over.

We surrendered the master bedroom to Roxy and Brett after persuading them to stay. Sioux Lookout police officers would never admit to anything white falling out of the sky in Toronto being the slightest obstacle.

We finally settled on an older bed we'd dragged into the downstairs rec room. Then lay in the quiet and the dark watching the snow drift to earth through an elevated window.

"The Miles thing is over now, right?" Kate said.

"Yeah, it's over." We closed our eyes.

November, 2019, a sunny Tuesday in Samana, Dominican Republic

Tony leaned in, "Check out those two." I sighed.

"Be your age, Tony." But I still looked up at the pair of women entering the bus.

I noticed the odd combination of similarities and differences. Both appeared to be in their middle thirties. Both were dark and attractive.

The first onboard was short, lean; athletic looking; with pixie-cut black hair and fierce unnaturally large brown eyes. She wore shorts and a pink tee that didn't suit her. Her legs were attractive but muscular for a woman

The second, taller and curvier, had a softer expression on her face. I still thought *athlete* as she passed.

Tony turned and watched them walking down the aisle.

"Don't be such a fucking perv," I said in a stage whisper. "You have two weeks to ogle women on the beach."

He leaned back in the seat and turned his face towards mine. "It's not what you think; okay, a bit what you think, but did you notice anything about the short one?"

"What about her? She had really big eyes and walked with authority. It wouldn't surprise me if she had some military training."

"Yes, I mean no; you know what I mean."

"Oh good God, you think she's evil."

"She is, but she has just enough good in her to put it on a knife edge. I've never seen anything like it. You want to keep an eye on that one."

I glanced back. "What about the other one?"

"There's something about her too…"

"You got another beer in that bag?"

Yes, one year later, we were back, on our way to the same resort. I watched the sunlight dappling through the palm fronds, felt the heat, and began to relax.

Brenda had generated this idea. Arguably the wisest among us, she had suggested during a summer barbeque at their home in Kingston that the best way to put Miles death behind us would be to return and experience… nothing, just an ordinary resort.

If it hadn't come from her, and especially if it had come from me, Kate would have resisted. I was surprised, then as I considered her decision, not surprised.

When I met Kate she had been smart mouthed and cocky but more innocent than she appeared on the surface. Her father, a fiercely aggressive criminal lawyer, was the personification of loving warmth at home. Her mother, right up until her death was an amiable woman with an ill kept secret but somewhat managed love of hard liquor.

Years working with testosterone poisoned business execs had taken much of the shine off her and the big blow came when I cheated on her with a client and saw my career go up in smoke.

And then there were the murders in Sioux Lookout…

It could be argued that we were both better people for our struggles; which are, after all, inevitable in life. Our marriage was solid; we would never divorce and time rendered us softer and more loving towards each other.

We had all been shaken up by Miles death; more than we thought at the time. No one had PTSD or anything but witnessing the remains of a sordid end cast a pall on our lives.

Roxy had called after Christmas and told me about their visit with Carter Miles. An only child, he was rattled by the relatively early deaths of both his parents. But he was in a good marriage himself, had children and was handling the aftermath as well as could be expected.

They had found him at home with his wife, kids and a buddy; everyone he needed for support.

I hoped Roxy would dig deeper and I think she tried but Carter couldn't tell them much. He was as confused as everyone else.

"When I called, he was usually sober; and when I visited too," he told Brett and my daughter. They were all sitting in his living room with coffee.

"But I was getting calls from cops all the time about him being around town and drunk. It didn't make sense. He was never much of a drinker when I was young, just the occasional beer. I don't think he even liked booze."

Roxy couldn't make sense of that and neither could I.

In the end the conversation had come around to me.

"I'm glad you're a cop and we're on the same team, Roxane. One thing I don't think my dad ever did was tell your dad how much he appreciated his detective skills." Roxy groaned.

"I've been hearing those war stories my whole life. I'm glad he didn't tell dad that. His head would explode."

I made her tell me the whole conversation in the end.

"My head won't explode," I told her.

Flashback to a barbeque

I sort of let Miles death go but it played on our minds. So when we started all talking about Miles during a barbeque in Kingston, Brenda spoke out.

They had bought a nice suburban house with a deck after the shooting. Tony, following some sort of incident effecting his twins, let the Silver Birch housing project go and embraced domesticity.

Our grandson, Liam, had been born, and we arrived with two bottles of good champagne to celebrate.

"Now you've done, it Chris," Tony said. "That stuff goes right to Brenda's head."

"It makes everyone feel good," I said.

"Oh, better than good in my case," Brenda said darkly.

With that strange benediction we spent an evening on their deck, under the apple tree, listening to the night sounds and laughing, maybe a little hysterically.

"Okay," Tony said, "you brought a night bag for the guest room, and the champagne; so why drag that knapsack onto the deck?"

"Something inside I want to show you."

Kate chuckled. "Marie-Giselle would say that every family therapist alive is a drama queen; come on Chris, show him what's in the bag."

Tony laughed. "She's right about that. I remember her." He switched to a painful version of mom's accent:

"Ah, the inuiteeve from' the 'rung side of the tracks. You always meees' your mother and try to manage with the vodka, but marrieeed the perfect woman my son so carelessly discarded..."

We laughed guiltily, except Kate, the woman for whom Brenda had been discarded. But the crepuscular dark had encroached and Tony was not deterred. "What's in the bag, buddy?"

"A copy of the Scarborough Mirror," I said, naming a commercial rag that showed up on doorsteps all over Scarberia.

"So?" I reached into the bag and retrieved the paper and handed it to him. He plucked reading glasses from his shirt front and read the cover.

"Holy fucking shit, they're tearing down Silver Birch." All eyes were on Tony. He had grown up in that particular dump then worked there as a social worker for thirty years.

He didn't hesitate and raised his glass.

"A toast to Silver Birch, good fucking riddance, and here's to whatever future slum they build in its place." We drank.

Later, after mosquitos chased us indoors, we sat on the oxblood leather furniture that spoke to Brenda's alarming taste in décor, drinking brandy.

"Anybody still freaked out about Miles?" I asked.

"I am," Brenda said. "And I'm the only one here who didn't know him. I've seen my share of bad stuff, but this got under my skin."

"Kind of spoils a beach vacation, finding a corpse," Kate said. "I love the tropical getaway thing but I'm reluctant to go this year."

I shrugged. "We need to go somewhere else and put it behind us. Old age is about leaving things behind anyway. This year we go to Cuba or Mexico."

"We're still talking beaches, palm trees, rum punch, antacids, the trots, sunburn and all of that," she said.

"No, let's all go back to the same Resort." We stared at Brenda. I saw Tony nod and Kate's head tilt.

"Really?" she said.

"Sure, Sunbeams Samana was great. Beautiful place overlooking the Bay; friendly staff, decent food, why not? It will be in our face for one day, then we can toast Miles and carry on."

We retired not long after, and woke the next morning with hangovers and a plan.

Back to Samana on a Tuesday morning, Kate

I would have been upset watching those idiots gawk at younger women 20 years ago. Now I treat it as a reflex in two silly old men who, on balance, have done more for the world than against it.

We've taken the two hour run down the highway to Kingston more often this year and become closer to Tony and Brenda.

I have never had a problem with Tony. He was always – and remains – a boozy horndog with a good heart. He's done some strange things; I don't pretend to understand, but Brenda is always there with him.

She's changed; I don't know how exactly, but sometimes an angry gleam appears in her eyes. Ah, what the hell, we are on vacation. That is the whole point, isn't it? To have nothing to do with last year.

It won't work. Of course we will. Fucking social workers; so decent, so full of shit.

Fancy drinks in the lobby

Tonight was Caipirinha night in the lobby and a few lovely Dominican women were set up with Cachaça and various accoutrement. Tony and I were sent into the crowd with instructions to return with delicious drinks or die trying.

As we edged our way out with the drinks we found Kate and Brenda sitting at a table with another couple. There was no room for us and they barely looked up when we deposited the hard won cocktails.

We looked around for another table and found one half occupied by the bar. We found ourselves sitting with the two women we had ogled earlier on the bus.

"Hey, look who it is," said the shorter of the two. "The horny old men who checked us out on the bus." The taller one slapped her forehead. But I heard the accent and responded to the first woman with my best Parisian accent:

"Que ferions-nous d'autre en présence de si belles femmes?" She laughed.

"Maintenant tu' baises avec moi..." she said, in a true Quebecois joual.

It worked; we laughed, though Tony and the other women didn't know what we said.

"Marie, show some manners," said the tall woman.

"Chris, fuck off with the French," Tony said. I smiled.

"Hi, my name is Chris Allard," I said. This was fun; but I glanced over to see if Kate was watching. Satisfied she wasn't, I carried on, speaking to the tall one. "I think I recognize your accent." She raised her eyebrows.

"Okay, where am I from."

"Scarberia,"

"Very Good! We have a winner."

"I'm from Scarborough too," Tony said. "I'm Tony Price."

"Courtney Snow. Nice to meet you." She extended her hand to shake ours.

"My name is Marie Lesage," said the other woman, "and I am not from Scarborough." We laughed again. That much, so obvious. "I am from Chicoutimi."

We all laughed some more, probably because of the weird conversation, impotent sexual tension and the fact that we were all drunk.

Now Kate looked over, and Brenda too.

"Why are you drinking those pussy cocktails?" Marie said.

"Is that a mixed drink?" I asked. She sat with a tall glass, quarter filled with a dark liquid, in front of her.

"Extra proof rum, straight up," she said. I shuddered but Tony grinned.

"You're my kind of girl! Want another?"

"Go for it handsome stranger!" I looked at Courtney and realized that we were fellow travelers with the two craziest people in the room.

"Aren't you going to introduce us?" Kate appeared with Brenda, just as Tony, once more headed into the fray.

"This is Courtney," I said, "and Marie."

"Nice to meet you. "I'm Kate and this is Brenda." Then she frowned. "You're not social workers?"

Both younger women shook their heads as Tony returned bearing a tray laden with tall glasses of viscous brown liquid.

"I got the good stuff from the bar guy. Hi Kate, don't worry about Chris, he's too fucking old to hit on young chicks."

"I just turned 37," Marie said with a frown.

"Young chicks," Tony repeated. "Chris just turned 67." I glared at him. Marie already had her hands on one of the glasses.

"You can hang out if you bring drinks," she said.

"We'll save you some seats by the music," Kate said with a smile. She could afford to be smug. Tony was right; married social workers closing on seventy were the acme of unthreatening.

I took a sip of my drink; things were beginning to swirl around the room, between the booze and noise.

"So what do you guys do?"

"We hunt large fish," Marie said, with a giggle. "We just caught – after two years of trying – a gigantic octopus."

"Congrats," I said. Okay. They fished.

"Real monster?" Tony asked. His rum was almost gone. Be interesting to see him and Marie go head to head in a drinking contest.

"You have no idea," Marie continued, "it..." Courtney whacked her on the arm. I think she did that a lot. But Marie didn't seem to mind.

"I'm an Ichthyologist," she said. "Marie's in the navy."

"So you are researchers."

"More hunter/killers..." I glanced nervously towards the ocean.

"What the fuck you doing taking a seaside vacation?" Tony said. "Wouldn't it make more sense to go to Saskatchewan or something? Both women laughed.

"It was her idea," Marie said. A bird squawked from the rafters. It had flown into the atrium by mistake and decided to stay and cadge crumbs.

"We sit on the beach for a couple of weeks, maybe meet some handsome men and get some action." Courtney closed her eyes, likely in supplication to some unseen power that might shut her friend up.

"That's what I did at your age," Tony said. "Went on beach vacations to screw women in the insurance industry." My eyes casually met with Courtney's. Nothing flirty, more silent acknowledgement of our crazy friends.

"Hey buddy," I said out loud to Tony before he managed to embarrass me further, "someone's going to be downstairs hitting on our wives. Courtney and Marie, it was great to meet you both. Thanks for the laughs."

"Likewise," Marie said. We left.

On the way down the steps to the pool I spoke to Tony. "Those are two weird chicks."

"Kinda hot, though, aren't they?"

"Oh yeah."

Breakfast on a beautiful morning

Kate and I were the early birds of the foursome. And given the drinking and general hedonism of the all-inclusive holiday everyone should be allowed to crawl back to consciousness at their own rate.

Tony and Brenda had always started work early where Kate and I had flexibility. Let them sleep in.

When I decided to start the day with a Mimosa Kate raised her eyebrows.

"We social workers have a rep for being unctuous and sanctimonious; I need to set the record straight."

"Nothing says that like drinking alone at breakfast."

The server had been by with cutlery and glasses of water. But while we were kibitzing someone put two more glasses in front of us.

"Everyone's hung over and they're trying to rehydrate us," I said.

"Well, thanks to them!" Kate picked up the new glass and drank it down.

"You should drink water too, especially if you're trying to keep up with Tony all week."

"There's orange juice in the Mimosa."

"Have it your own way, Chris. You'll be like Tony at the end of two weeks."

"Tall and handsome?"

"He's lucky his liver doesn't show."

"What a tale it could tell."

We were still laughing when we returned to the room to get ready for the beach.

Kate forgets the sunscreen

I couldn't find the sun screen. I thought I had packed it in the beach bag with the paperbacks, crossword books, reading glasses and other things. We'd managed to score some good seats under the shade of a palm, carefully stripped of coconuts to avoid braining tourists.

Chris fetched himself a beer; it was still too early for me to drink.

"Chris, you stay here; we're going to burn on our first day if we're not careful. I'm going to trek back to the room; see you in a bit."

A shadow falls

Kate was taking her time getting back from the room; I wondered if she'd run into Tony and Brenda. Even though I kept repositioning the beach chair to fall under the shade, I knew that I would eventually have to apply sunscreen or face the consequences.

Our new friends, Courtney and Marie strolled by and waved. I still thought they were an odd couple. I didn't get a gay vibe from them but who knew. What was that bullshit last night about a giant octopus?

I decided to get the sun screen myself. No point ruining the vacation with a burn on the first day.

When I returned to the room it smelled curiously fishy and uncomfortable. I looked around and saw Kates bag and the sunscreen sitting on the desk. The maid hadn't been through yet and the money we left her was untouched. The bathroom door was closed.

"Hey Kate, you okay?"

"Chris?" The tone was weak and all wrong.

"What's the matter?" I said through the bathroom door.

"I'm sick."

"Got the runs?" Silence. "Hey hon." She didn't respond. The door was open and I went in. She was sitting on the toilet but her eyes were closed and breathing shallow.

I went to my knees in front of her and cupped her face; her skin felt cold and clammy. The floor was damp with some kind of clear fluid. She moaned but kept her eyes closed.

Many of us get the trots on vacation. You eat the wrong thing and next thing you know you're on the pot. You swallow an anti-diarrheal and move on.

This was different. I wrapped a clean towel around her and moved directly to the phone.

"We need a doctor right away for room 307," I said to the operator. "My wife is very ill." He didn't respond and I waited through a long pause. But he was checking something out.

"Excuse me sir, Dr. Fernando just left the building. I will attempt to contact him on his cell phone. Please stay in your room."

I returned to Kate who sat uneasily on the toilet.

"Sweetheart, they're calling the doctor…" The phone rang and the operator told me he'd contacted the doctor and he should be by in 15 minutes.

He arrived in 10. Kate had said little. I just stayed in front holding her steady. I heard the knock on the door.

A slim handsome black man stood by the door holding an old fashioned medical bag. He was on the high side of six feet, and wore a baby blue sea island shirt with tortoise shell glasses.

"Hey dude, nice to meet you," he said in perfect unaccented English, "Mark Fernando. Let's get a boo at the lady."

Hey dude? Had they sent the surfing instructor by mistake? But he was already in the room and headed towards the bathroom. I followed. He introduced himself to Kate while placing his bag on the counter and reaching in for a pair of latex gloves.

He looked over the situation and frowned. "Can you help me get her onto the bed? It will be easier for me to examine her. I nodded. "Ma'am, your hubby is going to help me get you over to the bed; I'm going to need you to help us out."

Kate still didn't speak but nodded. After we laid her down he went back into the bathroom to inspect the contents of the toilet.

"When did this start?" he asked me.

"She was fine a couple of hours ago, after breakfast." We lay her down and he went to work with his examination. I had to answer most of the questions.

"Do you know what her blood pressure usually is?" he asked after removing the cuff.

"Pretty normal, 120 over 80, I think." He didn't respond but looked at her, frowned, then spoke to me again.

"You got insurance?" I glanced at the safe where we stored the papers.

"Yeah." I named the company. "We're careful about that."

"Sorry to ask, but it will make everything easier, Mr. Allard."

"Chris."

"Chris, I think I know what's happening here, but I need to get the missus to the International clinic in Samana right away and run a few tests on her – and you – and start treatment."

"Do it." Mark picked up the phone and made a few calls, delivering orders in rapid fire Spanish with what, to my ears, sounded like a Dominican accent.

After explaining what was about to happen to Kate who looked scared and subdued, he spoke to me.

"The ambulance should be here in about half an hour. We're going to get Kate on a saline drip right away and send her to the hospital. If you want you can come with me. Grab those insurance papers out of the safe. You're going to need them."

"Sure, thanks." The morning had started with a Mimosa and by lunchtime I was in Mark's car barreling down the road full speed.

"Why do you want to test me?" I said, as he swerved to avoid a skinny dog.

"I think you are okay; but it's prudent to check, man."

"Where did you go to med school?" I asked, as casually as I could. I didn't want to get on the bad side of this guy but I was curious.

"I did med school and my internal medicine residency at UCLA, Geffen School of medicine."

"Are you Dominican?"

"I'm from Los Angeles; my parents are Dominican and I was raised with the language and culture." Mark had also picked up some California culture along the way.

But he was okay with my enquiry. A lifetime of asking nosy questions made them come naturally from my mouth.

"My parents sacrificed a lot to make me a doctor. All they asked in return is that I practice in the Dominican Republic three months a year."

"They want to give back…"

"The family always claimed my dad was the dumbest guy in the village, I think sending his doctor son back is his way of saying, "fuck you.""

Okay.

"But *I* want to give back."

He tilted his head at a couple of kids by the side of the road, "I treat people like you so I can treat people like them." Fair enough. But he had a question for me, "What's your line of work, Chris?"

"I'm a social worker."

"Okay, so you get the treating the poor thing."

"Of course."

This didn't seem the right moment to tell him that my last client was majority shareholder in a sporting goods franchise, so I sat back and held on to the seat. Mark might be an all American guy but he drove like a Dominican.

They were just moving Kate into a private room when we arrived. Mark excused himself and sent me to a wait room. Not long after a grim looking nurse arrived and took me to a consulting room to be poked, prodded and swabbed.

I sat alone in the Wait room after; regretting leaving my reading glasses behind. It was nearly 3 when Mark returned.

He said down and said, "Everything's cool, man and Kate's going to be fine but I have some things to tell you." I felt a tear forming at the corner of my eye.

Goddam the tears. I hated growing old. But his next statement came as a shock.

"Kate has cholera." I sat up in my seat and took a breath.

"That's a serious disease, isn't it?"

"It is." He paused to put his words together. "You don't have it by the way, Chris. No sign of the bacterium at all. Treating cholera isn't rocket science; it's quite treatable. The trick is getting to it right away. And we did. Left too long, people die."

I shuddered.

"I want to keep Kate in hospital overnight on fluids. We've started her on antibiotics as well. She should be lots better tomorrow. In fact, as long as she keeps it low key, stays hydrated and avoids alcohol you can finish out your vacation."

"How did she get it?" Mark sat back in his chair.

"That's a mystery, Chris. I called the hotel a few minutes ago. No one else has reported being sick; a few cases of mild diarrhea but there always are. We have had problems with cholera in Haiti and the DR for years but it doesn't often show up in the resorts.

"It would have almost certainly been picked up through food or water but I have no idea where."

"What's even stranger, she's a healthy woman who went zero to ninety in a few hours. Her system was flooded with the bacterium. No idea how that happened."

I took a breath. "Thanks," I said.

"No worries. Oh by the way, no problemo with your insurance; everything's covered. The hotel has put you in a new room so they can sterilize the old one, and moved your stuff. They're sending a car to take you back. In the meantime I think a short visit with your wife is in order."

"Shouldn't I stay?"

"Nope, I want her and you to rest tonight. We'll send her back tomorrow and everything should be cool."

Kate, on her visit with Chris.

I don't know why Chris always thinks I am going to be mad at him. And of course he had to start with a wisecrack.

"You should have started the day with a Mimosa darling." He was glancing around the room. It looked, clean, white and antiseptic; well equipped, like any good hospital room anywhere.

"Very funny." But tears were forming in my eyes. "Thanks for calling the doctor right away."

"You looked awful Kate."

"I felt like I was going to die." No point giving him a hard time.

"How the hell did I get cholera? Did the doctor saying anything?"

Chris shrugged. It's funny how things can turn around. I had felt like I was on the edge of death. Now I just felt like sleeping.

"Mark has no idea."

"Mark?" Okay, at least Chris hadn't yet pissed him off.

"He's a good guy. I'm glad he was around."

"We were joking about keeping hydrated this morning when they brought that extra water," I said. But Chris was tuning out, like something had distracted him. This must have been scary for him.

"Anyway, you're fine, you son of a bitch. Go back and get drunk with Tony and Brenda tonight."

"Kate, what a thing..."

"Chris, it worked out. We're good. Go and let me sleep this off." A formal looking nurse poked her head into the room.

"Senor Allard, your car is here." He blew me a kiss and left. I don't think a real kiss would have given him cholera but at least now I can sleep.

At the bar with Tony and Brenda

"What in the fuck happened, Chris?" Tony said.

"How's Kate?" Brenda said.

They both met me at the door.

"I need a drink," I said.

"Yes you do." Tony was already steering me towards a table in the lobby by the bar.

When we had settled and he had fetched everyone rum punch, I told them the story.

"Cholera!" Tony said. They were shocked. "We used to have a doctor neighbor who treated cholera in Haiti."

"I don't remember you mentioning him."

"He wasn't around long; Brenda threw him off the roof of Kingston General." Brenda gave him a sharp dig in the ribs with her elbow.

"Tony, you want to watch the jokes, man."

"Yes," Brenda agreed with me. She took the conversation out of Tony's hands.

"How did she get it? This isn't just the usual trots." The rum was starting to work on my system and I shared my fear.

"You know how they give you water when you sit at a table in the buffet? Was it my imagination or were the staff looking over? It only now occurred to me how disturbing this event must be for them.

"This morning we sat, the water was poured and then someone – I didn't see who – brought two more glasses. Does that make sense?"

"So you think someone deliberately gave you…," Brenda paused and lowered her voice, "the germs in a glass of water? How come you didn't get sick?"

I took a pull from the rum. Tony looked over at the bartender and made a gesture involving a pouring motion with one hand

and an invisible glass with the other. The bartender nodded. Tony could be quite charming, but he shared a special rapport with those who served liquor. And he tipped well.

"I had a Mimosa for breakfast." She nodded.

"Even if that's true, why would anyone want to poison Kate?"

"Maybe someone was trying to poison Chris," Tony said. "That would make more sense." Brenda nodded.

"Thanks, Tony."

"Who hasn't wanted to kill you at some point?" Brenda chuckled. I looked down at my drink; not too sweet. The punch drinks were usually syrupy. Tony continued:

"Did you tell anyone that you thought Miles was murdered last year?"

"I didn't exactly say that, did I?" I paused for a minute, "Maybe a few people." I swallowed what was left in the glass.

"What if the wrong person thought you were here investigating the murder?"

"I have no good reason to think Miles was murdered. And even so, why would I come back a year later? It would make no sense - talk about a cold trail; all the visitors are new and probably a lot of the staff.

"Besides, who here would know I have ever investigated anything?" Another tear formed in my eye. "Damn, I must be losing it while Kate is sitting in the hospital."

We finished our drinks and after a bit, wandered down to the buffet. It was Dominican night and someone said they would be serving local dishes.

Tony and Brenda also made me promise to come to the Michael Jackson show by the pool; they didn't want me sitting alone in the room. I gave Kate a last thought and surrendered to the flow.

Thursday morning, Courtney Snow wanders the beach

I could kill Marie right now; what was I thinking travelling here with that crazy bitch?

A few moments back I passed a guy in his late twenties arguing with his wife, standing over their beach chairs; a handsome dude with dark curly hair and a smile that often traded places with confusion.

I noticed that last night after returning to the room and finding Marie and him returning at the same time.

"Hey girlfriend, I need half an hour to fuck this guy," she said before closing the door in my face.

I don't care if she wants to have sex on vacation but would it have been too much trouble to process it for a moment; maybe ask if it's okay to oust me from the room.

And half an hour? What was her idea of sex?

Throwing my hands up, I returned to the bar and chatted with a few folks. A rumour was going around that someone had gotten sick and it was infectious.

Nobody looked sick and the scientist in me dismissed it as overblown.

I found my new buddies Chris and Tony sitting with Brenda, Tony's wife, and joined them.

"Where's Marie?" Tony asked, "Fucking some guy in the room?"

Chris rolled his eyes and Brenda laughed. I looked closer at Tony; I can usually tell if someone has a psychic gift; and there it was.

"Where's Kate?" I asked Chris, skipping both Tony's question and too accurate guess. Moments later I was glad I did.

"In hospital with cholera," he said.

"Holy shit, how quickly did they get to it?"

"Quickly, she's going to be fine and I don't think anyone else is going to get it." He looked at me closely. "You know anything about cholera and how to prevent it?"

"I studied bacteriology during my doctoral studies, but mostly to poison invasive species." I checked myself. That wouldn't cheer him up and Chris must be having a bad night. "So, it's not systemic, the bacterium; in the water or food or anything?"

"No, seems to be a one off."

Brenda turned to Chris. "She's back tomorrow isn't she?"

"Yeah, she's going to stay on antibiotics for a bit and avoid booze but supposedly she'll be fine."

"I'm happy to hear that, Chris. When you see her wish her the best from me and Marie." I made a face. "My room should be free now. 'Night." I left but I was puzzled; how did one person get cholera that fast?

"I'll walk you to the elevator," Chris said. "I have to find my new quarters and call the girls to let them know what happened to their mom."

"You okay?" I asked him as we waited for the elevator to arrive.

"Courtney, does it seem strange to you that someone would get sick with cholera that quickly – and just one person?"

"I'm not an expert, but yeah it does." The elevator arrived; we travelled up a couple of floors and went our separate ways.

Marie looked like the cat that ate the canary when I poked my head in the room.

"You alone?"

"Yes, girlfriend." Ugh, I hated it when she called me that. It always sounded so wrong coming out of her mouth. I had planned to tell her about Chris' wife and *not* ask about her… *whatever*, but realized I was mad and decided to go to bed.

Neither of us were particularly upset with each other in the morning. We were civil and Marie somehow found the restraint to *not* say what I knew she was thinking: *You're just jealous.*

If she had I'd have thrown her off the bloody balcony.

Because she would have been right. I had a boyfriend, but for some good reasons, it was not physical, and the deprivation was making me crazy.

So now I wandered the beach to get some sun before diving again into the surf. The beach had filled quickly today; the day was glorious; hot, but not unbearably so.

Chairs and towels were filled with legions of the tubby, the white, and the middle aged. I could hear Russian, German, Italian and French being spoken in addition to English.

The waves ran high here; perhaps because the beach was so small and enclosed. It was fun but when I dove in I felt the menacing caress of the undertow.

Later, as I negotiated the water's edge a young woman approached from the opposite direction. She was black, wore her hair short and her bathing costume was a kind of long neutral shift.

"Morning," I said. She froze and stared.

Oh, God dammit. Courtney you idiot!

I was always doing this. And now I had just done it in a Spanish speaking locale. How would I wiggle out?

"You can see me," she said. They always started with that, but I was startled that she spoke English, though the accent was curious. I turned my body so that I was facing her, and looking out at the sea. Looking like you were talking to yourself was one of the hardest parts.

"Yes, I can," I said. "How are you today?"

"Fine, thank you." I took this part slowly. Most ghosts were angry, confused or mad as hatters. But her tone was kind of sweet. "My name is Lucy, what's yours?"

"Courtney." The preliminaries tend to go quickly. No one shook hands or exchanged hugs. "Lucy, how long have you been here?"

"About two hundred years, more or less."

"I'm sorry. You speak excellent English."

"I was a slave to English speaking people."

"I'm sorry."

"Don't be. Nothing much has changed. Coloured folks still work for white folks."

"Oh sure it has…" I stepped to one side; two black men in Sunbeams polo shirts staggered by carrying trays of drinks for a cluster of laughing matrons under a palm frond umbrella.

This was Lucy's view of the world – and those waiters. "Sorry, maybe not everywhere," I said lamely.

"Cheer up!" said, rather incongruously. "I am delighted to have met a friend who does not think I am invisible." She laughed. "Even when I was alive and working in the fields, I was invisible to white people."

"I'm sorry."

"You apologize too much, Courtney. You must be Canadian."

"Yes," I admitted. "How did you get here, Lucy?"

"Captain Reed was going to rape me so I fled into the waves."

"I'm…" She smiled.

"Don't say it, Courtney!" She had an infectious warmth. "That was a long time ago and…"

"You talking to a ghost?"

My heart nearly stopped. I whirled around and nearly hit Marie.

"You scared the shit out of me! And yes, I'm speaking to someone. Pretend to talk to me for a minute so I don't look like a total idiot." Marie gave me a thumbs up.

"Your girlfriend knows you talk to ghosts?" Lucy said. "She must be a very wise woman."

"She's a crazy sociopath," I said with feeling, not caring that Marie was there. "And you will never hear *her* apologise for anything."

"I hope we talk again, Courtney, and sometime I must introduce my companion and friend; he is Canadian too."

"You have a companion?" This seemed a small beach for more than one ghost. Marie didn't know which way to look but felt compelled to speak to Lucy.

"Her boyfriend's a ghost too. That's why she never gets any action."

"Marie! Nick and I have agreed to see other, ah, people and… ghosts." People thought being a medium was cool, but you spent much of your time looking and feeling stupid.

Lucy laughed again. "I will leave you two to resolve your differences."

After she left I glared at Marie. But she had approached me to provide cover for my talking to no one.

"Thanks." I said.

"You are welcome, girlfriend. Now come and get a beer with me so I can ogle another man. I think last night was a one-off with *le bel garcon*."

In the distance I could see *le bel garcon's* wife throwing a tube of sun screen at him.

Marie had recruited me as a naval monster chaser based on the unheard of combination of a doctorate in ichthyology and being gifted as a medium.

Real mediums were rare; most of the ones seen in public were frauds. One night last year my boyfriend Nick Herkimer had haunted me to attend a public reading in a "haunted" house by Madame Reynauld.

Lots of people came to enquire about their loved ones and as it turned out the house was haunted. The problem was that Madame Reynauld was making it all up.

The ghosts ran riot while she talked shit. They made bunny ears behind her head, told bad jokes and danced the twist in front of her.

"Faye, your husband Charlie is in the room," she said earnestly to one Kingston matron. "He has something to say…"

The ghosts started asking each other if anyone there was named Charlie. They thought it was hilarious. *"Is Charlie in the house? Oh Charlie, where are you?"*

One spectre finally said out loud: *"My name is Charlie. Ask Faye why she couldn't put out the occasional blowjob."*

Nick and I fell apart. No one could hear Nick laugh but I got thrown out. All the apparitions applauded as I was escorted to the door.

As Nick would say, Good times!

Oh well, running into ghosts came with the gift. Lucy seemed nice; maybe we could talk again.

Chris on Kate's return

In the end she was absent a little more than 30 hours. I had rarely seen her as subdued and vulnerable. She looked better but still pale. During the evening we provided her with bottled water and ordered from room service.

"They want me to eat and drink in the short run; it's better for me. And move around. But Chris, I think I just want to sit and watch the sun set."

"That's fine, Kate. Do you want Tony and Brenda to come by? They've been worried about you."

"I don't think I can face anyone yet, Chris. Grab a beer from the fridge and sit with me on the balcony." She made a face. "You know how every year you try and smoke a cigar? Don't."

"Wouldn't dream of it." Shortly after, facing into the western horizon, we were watched the late afternoon sun follow a long descending arc into the sea, leaving horizontal trails of Aurelian, vermilion and finally, indigo and black.

I sipped on my beer. I worried Kate was too hot in the sun but she didn't complain and worked away at the water bottle.

We ordered dinner and she turned to me.

"Chris, I am going to need a day or two to recover from this and I will be happy with food and drink and short strolls. I have lots of books and will appreciate check-ins but I want to you enjoy your vacation.

"Kate…"

"No seriously, hang out with Tony and Brenda, or even those weird girls from Canada, but have some fun."

Brenda Price

"This is all fucked," my husband stated, taking a long pull from a glass of dark rum on ice. We were sitting at a table overlooking the sea by the bar. Below us, a personable young man ran a bingo game by the pool.

I looked over. The game involved a clever set of floats that periodically dunked participants in the pool. I tried to remember if that would have ever been fun. These days I was content to be content.

If I had some work as a distraction, Tony had a monster, and the kids were okay; I was okay. But today Tony was running with Chris's theory that someone had poisoned Kate.

We had called the room to see if a visit would be okay but Chris told us to hold off for 24 hours. I could understand that. I knew Kate well enough to know that she would be embarrassed as well as queasy.

"I think you have to know Chris to want to poison him," he continued, "and since we're the only ones here who know him and we didn't do it, this is harder to fathom." Tony paused and took another drink. "Unless you did it, Brenda."

"Is that a question, Tony?" Someone screeched at the pool as they were dunked. He nodded.

"No, I didn't. I wanted to briefly in the 70's when she stole Chris but I'm over that."

"Okay, so you have a motive, but not a great one." I sighed.

"Tony, you're saying that the poison was intended for Chris?"

"Who would want to poison Kate, other than you a zillion years ago?"

"You're not making a lot of headway, Mr. Price." We both heard another screech and looked. The woman dunked this time lost her bikini top. Everyone cheered and clapped. She looked mortified as she scrambled to get it back on.

"Wow." Chris had arrived and was looking down at the pool.

"You guys never seen boobs before?"

"Not those ones," Tony said, with very masculine logic. "Hey Chris, we were trying to figure out who would poison Kate. I think the cholera stuff was meant for you."

You're probably right," he said glumly. "I don't have a clue. There's nothing to go on at all."

"Hey, why aren't you guys checking out the tits by the pool?"

"Marie!" The taller girl named Courtney glared at the other one. "Chris's wife is ill and you're asking him to look at other women?" Those two something-in-the-navy chicks had arrived. God, they were a strange pair.

"He obviously isn't getting any action and he's too old to fuck me…" Tony laughed so hard that his drink went right up through his nose. Not easily embarrassed, he reached for a napkin.

Chris blushed. I'm sure she meant well.

"Je pense que nous avons un boob ici," he said, in what I thought might be his version of a Quebecois accent. Either way, Marie laughed.

"We came by for a reason," Courtney said. She wore a light shirt over her bikini top. Nature had been generous with her. I glanced over to the boys. Tony and Chris were determined to keep their eyes north of the neckline.

With a certain kind of man, a woman never achieved more eye contact than when her boobs were on display. Checking them out was verboten to male social workers so both had long since learned to force propriety over natural inclination.

"There is a boat going out to that island tomorrow morning." She pointed and we all looked out, though only one large island lay in sight.

"We took the liberty of booking all four of you on the ride with us. It'll be fun; we'll get off the resort for a few hours."

"No way Kate's going out on the water," Chris said, "she's way too queasy. But she wants me to get out so sure." Courtney looked at me. I shrugged.

"Sure, count me and Tony in. Be fun to go for a boat ride."

The boat ride isn't fun

Fog had rolled in from Samana Bay, bringing a light chill that felt out of place in a tropical vacation.

I left Kate sitting with a Maeve Binchy paperback and half eaten breakfast, after packing a bag with my Rose coloured sweatshirt and other accoutrement. She had a view of the ocean.

"You want to go out into that?"

"The sun will burn it off. You sure you don't want to come?"

"Ugh."

With that benediction I set off down the stairs.

About ten of us met on the steps just outside the lobby to catch the shuttle to the dock. I said good morning to Courtney and Marie and sidled up to Brenda and Tony.

"Pirates will be waiting for us in a fog bank," Tony said.

"We're social workers; too poor to rob." Brenda said.

"They don't know that," Tony responded.

"They'll never guess that you're a social worker," I said to Tony. The tone was light though a whiff of trepidation hung in the air, excepting perhaps the two naval something chicks presumably accustomed to ocean life.

Later, while we stood on a dock, not far away Courtney said, apropos to nothing, "I hate boats." Tony laughed.

I had come to appreciate his sense of humour; it made him a great travel companion; he could find the funny in anything.

"I think Able Seaman Marie forgot to describe the naval work environment when she signed you up," he said.

Able Seaman Marie cast Tony a sidelong glance but didn't speak. We could hear gulls crying somewhere in the obscured sky. With the limits to our vision all sounds seemed exaggerated.

What the fuck was out there; Sharks, barracuda, Cthulhu? Or just the foreboding mystery that was the ocean.

Jesús was our Captain today and he waved us aboard an oldish 30 foot pilothouse boat. It took a few minutes and as soon as we were all aboard someone done up in a hoodie complained about feeling sick, and left.

Jesús shrugged and asked a boy on the dock to untie the rope and cast us off.

It was 9 am as we disappeared into the murk. Most of us wanted to cluster around the pilot for some reason; maybe to make sure he was doing his job. He showed no signs of distress as he steered the boat and pushed the throttle forward.

"His people have fished this bay for hundreds of years. He knows where he's going," Marie, also unfazed, said to no one in particular. We motored on into the gloom.

I'm not sure how much time passed, but no one anticipated the sharp flash and bang when it came. The steady hum of the inboard engine and our silence in the vaporous air made the shock worse as Jesús fell to his knees in front of the steering console, screaming in pain.

He briefly held onto the wheel before putting his hands to his eyes. He wasn't the only one. Two of the passengers also gasped, temporarily blinded by the bright light.

Throttle close to full, the small boat spun out of control.

Marie was on it in an instance; quickly asserting mastery over the throttle and wheel. We were lucky no one went over the side. Tony and Courtney were right beside her. Brenda put her arms around the injured captain.

As soon as the ship was put into neutral you could hear weeping; from pain and fear. I reached the console and asked, "What the fuck happened?"

"Look at this," Marie said, pointing to a scorch mark and melted plastic. "I think it's a small incendiary device. It must have gone off in the poor bastards face. And… fuck, do you hear that?"

We were briefly thrown off balance by the returning wake from our stop. Then she was pointing to the small cupboard under the console.

"Do you hear the ticking?" She didn't wait for an answer but threw the cheap doors open.

"Oh fuck," she said, repeating herself. But we all saw it. With the possible exception of her, we had only seen one of these in the movies but there was no mistaking the box, coloured wires and alarm clock wrapped in duct tape.

"It's a fucking bomb," Tony said.

"No shit, Sherlock," Marie said from her knees, "And it's set to go off in ten minutes."

"Christ, Marie, get rid of it!" Courtney said.

"Nope, we'll just set it off; I think it's C4; no we have to get rid of the passengers." Our shock must have shown but she had turned to face the stern and everyone on board.

"ATTENTION!" My name is Lieutenant Commander Marie Lesage of the Royal Canadian Navy and I am taking command of this vessel. Now hear this, do every fucking thing I say and you might live."

She had our attention.

"I am taking us to the island. We have just enough time. Everyone put on a lifejacket NOW, sit on the deck, and I will leave in 45 seconds."

Everyone did what they were told.

I sat beside Tony and Brenda.

"*Able seaman Marie*," I hissed to Tony. He shrugged and smiled. The bastard was having fun.

Time runs out, Courtney

What a fucking mess! But we had no time to think; Marie was functioning on instinct and experience. At the 45 second mark she hit the throttle, banked the boat and pushed it to max. Everyone sat cowed and terrified behind us.

If anything the fog was thicker in the open water.

"Do you have any fucking idea where you're going?" I asked over the roar of the engine, "In a few minutes the boat blows to bits"

"Relax girlfriend, I had a glance at the chart. A couple of seconds anyway; that's all I needed." As if to demonstrate, she made a quick half turn of the wheel that nearly knocked me off my pins. "Buoy," she explained.

"The chart was up to date but I am going to have to take a guess around the sand bars." Her ridiculous baseball cap had flown off and now her hair lifted madly in the wind.

After a soaking of salt spray, I turned to join the others on the deck but she grabbed my arm.

"We're going to slow down and stop in a sec and I'm going to need you," she said.

"For what?" But she was already throttling back. I didn't see a thing except more of this goddam fog.

She turned again to the passengers. *"ATTENDEZ! We are all going over the side, me first and Brenda Price last."* Brenda Price? How did she make that decision? Brenda seemed nice enough but Marie knew I was the strongest swimmer.

People started to talk but she ruthlessly cut them off. "You will follow me to the south southeast. Paddle gently and let the waves carry you. I have dead reckoning and won't miss. The sand will be under your feet in 50 meters and the shore 50 meters after that. Understand?" She turned to me:

"You're staying, girlfriend. Take off your life jacket."

"What! You're the goddam Captain, you be last off the fucking ship!"

"We don't have time for this Courtney." (*Courtney!* Now I was worried.) "If I don't lead the group some of them are going to get lost and drown. As soon as we are off, you are going to turn the vessel around and gun it out to sea…"

"Have you lost your fucking mind?"

"Count slowly to 30, ease the throttle then jump. Dive as deep as you can and swim to shore." She made it sound like a sunfish level swimming lesson.

"You crazy bitc..."

But she was gone, leaving me at the wheel. In seconds, everyone was over the side, including a teenage girl that Marie had to grab by her hair and shorts and toss into the drink.

As soon as I saw Brenda swim beyond the reach of the propeller I hit it... off, into the void... Dear God...

Tension and weirdness onshore

We made it. I'm grateful but it all happened so quickly; I don't know what to think. Most of us were thrown onto the sandbar by the explosion. And it was huge. We had seen Courtney drive the boat into the fog and with the lifejackets it wasn't a difficult swim but now we were deafened as well as half blinded.

It sounded much louder than it would in a movie.

Brenda paddled round back while Marie shouted deprecations at the passengers.

"Swim you dumb bitch!"

"Tony you lazy prick, kick your legs."

I was first onshore and turned to help others. Brenda emerged pulling the teenager by the loop on her life jacket. She had been a gifted athlete when she was young, and even while looking old ladyish now she was strong as hell.

Marie was last out of the water. She took one glance back and started shouting more orders.

"Everyone together by that tree. We're going to sing."

People, still dripping and shaken, appeared confused. But Tony, still breathing hard, got it right away. "C'mon, let's go!"

"Even *maudit Anglais* know *Frère Jacques*. All together now!" Marie began.

The two Germans onboard looked baffled but they'd pick it up. I'd figured out what we were doing now but Marie started.

"FRERE JACQUES..."

We sang:

> *Frère Jacques,*
> *Dormez-vous ?*
> *Sonnez les matines !*
> *Ding, daing, dong !*

"Louder Godammit! Sing!"

We sang as loud as we could. The terrified teen tried to flee but Brenda again grabbed her by the scruff. Adrenalin screamed through our bodies. We gulped for breath. Tears ran down from our eyes.

This was probably futile...

She emerged, topless, breasts heaving, long black hair dripping from her shoulders, like a Goddess of the deep... And she was pissed. She spotted Marie.

"You fucking psycho! "You crazy cu..."

Marie pumped her fist in the air. "Hooray for Courtney Snow!" She saved the day! Hip hip hooray!" We all let out a cheer.

Courtney gave up. She turned, flopped down on her back in the sand and lay still. For a moment we wondered if she had dropped dead. But after a quick breath, she spoke:

"Does someone have something I can put on?"

"I do." I unzipped my sweatshirt. It was wet but would do the job.

Kate, later, back in the room

Say what you want, this isn't shaping into a dull vacation. My historical first urge, confronted with another of Chris' outre adventures would be to get mad and blame him.

But I love him and have learned to control my tongue. Good God; a bomb, a swim to the beach, an explosion, a naked ichthyologist!

They had all piled into the room, Chris, Tony and Brenda; wired on adrenalin, pouring out the story. They drank all the miniatures of liquor in the fridge then tumbled out again, leaving a sandy floor behind them.

Chris says that a teenager managed to save her cell phone from mortal danger, they found a signal and the Samana police came to the island and escorted them home. Everyone was shaken but thanks to Marie and Courtney, no one was hurt, except the pilot who is in hospital being treated for facial burns.

The cops praised those navy chicks but pooh-poohed the bomb theory. They said the explosion was probably the result of a cigarette and leaking gas line.

But they all saw the bomb.

Someone tried to kill them and almost got away with it. If everyone had been blown to bits on the ocean it would have been attributed to a leak and the story would be over.

In the bar

"Kate getting cholera is bad. But today almost a dozen people could have been killed in order to kill me."

"We don't know that, Chris," Brenda said. I was twisting a glass of beer around in my hands.

Adrenalin and near death experiences are like a stimulant drug; you feel elated and terrified at the same time. And horny, if Kate wasn't sick… I tried to calm myself down. "I feel badly for that driver."

"I didn't get the impression that he was going to lose his sight but maybe we can check with someone tomorrow and find out how he is." Brenda leaned forward. "This isn't your fault, Chris."

"It feels like it."

"You didn't plant the damn bomb," Tony said. The elation I felt was troubling to me, even though Brenda seemed unfazed and

Tony happy as a lark. I knew all kinds of clinical responses but right now I wanted to drink it away.

"What's the matter with the police here anyway? We all saw the bomb. A naval officer saw the bomb. They use bombs in the navy! They don't believe us." I took a long gulp of beer. It tasted better than usual today.

"I don't know about that," Tony said.

"What did you see?" Brenda said. She was sipping something sweet and pink.

"That one cop, the quiet one. I watched him. He was writing the whole time Marie described the bomb. I think it's more a matter of not acknowledging than not believing."

"How did it even get *on* the boat?" I asked out loud. I needed to be careful. I tended to raise my voice when agitated.

"It couldn't have been anyone on the boat," Brenda noted. "The bomber wasn't going to blow himself up." She paused and turned to Tony, "You didn't feel anything evil did you?"

"Other than Marie? Funny, I thought I did on the way to the dock but tuned it out. After, when we were altogether on that beach I did a quick scan. Nothing."

"Someone got off the boat," Brenda said.

"Wait, I remember," I took another swallow. I am usually a moderate drinker but tonight... it would be a good night to get drunk. "Do you guys remember someone getting off the boat just as we were about to leave? Said they were sick or something?"

"Yes," Brenda remembered. "I do, but nothing about them."

"Man or woman?" She shrugged. We tried for a while but none of us could remember details.

Before my boozy thrash could get into gear fatigue caught up with me. Between the swimming, excitement and grog, my body started to fall from under me.

We broke up and the old social workers went home to bed.

Saturday on the beach

Dr. Fernando arrived early.

"Hey bro," he said to me at the door. I guess we were friends. "Gotta have a chat with the wife. Kate okay?"

"Yeah, still a bit subdued, but okay. He walked in with his bag, waving to Kate and setting up at the desk in the room. I still had things I wanted to know. "Anyone else sick?"

"No, just her. It's weird, man; one person, no discernable source. It happens but we can usually at least take a good guess." Kate was laying herself down for whatever he was going to do. But I thought I would risk one more question.

"Do you know how that guy, Jesús is doing after the bomb?"

"I didn't hear anything about a bomb," he said, too quickly. He turned away from me and found something else to look for in his bag. "I have a few calls to make this morning," he said. He moved towards Kate then glanced back to answer me.

"Jesús is okay. A few superficial burns; he'll be seeing bright lights for a bit but there's no ocular trauma." I didn't push it but stepped back. He checked a few things out on his cowed patient, asked some questions and pronounced her well.

"Thanks Mark," I said as he left.

"No worries, bro, glad this had a happy ending." He paused, as if there was something else he wanted to say, then walked out the door.

"Did he seem strange to you," I said to Kate, who remained on the bed.

"In the same room as you, Chris? How would I even notice? Did you notice he said I was well now?"

"That's great, Kate. I have some thinking to do. You ready for the beach?"

"Tomorrow, Chris. Now leave me alone."

I left her with books and some food. I still felt guilty but I also understood when she insisted. She told me that with all the frightening stuff going on she felt peaceful in the room.

Tony and Brenda were not in evidence on the beach so I pulled a long chair into a shady spot by the stone retaining wall, lay down the towel, sunk a plastic cup of beer into the sand and opened my book.

I was distracted; by the high surf, the polyglot conversations, the bodies in bikinis and my thoughts. All this crazy shit on a vacation and here I was sitting with a beer, content.

A shadow fell across my space and I looked to the side. The shadow belonged to the woman who had saved our lives yesterday. She looked down over me and tilted her head.

"Hi Courtney," I said.

"Chris, we need to talk."

Everything gets stranger still

She dragged a plastic chair through the sand, and sat down on the side facing me. I tilted the headrest on my chaise longue and scootched forward. A small green lizard appeared at the bottom of an adjacent Palm, as if it wanted in on the conversation.

She looked serious and a bit nervous, as if she didn't know where to start. Had I said something wrong? Oh God, she was mad that I looked at her boobs yesterday.

She surprised me.

"Would you know if someone had schizophrenia?"

"Marie go off her meds?" This was a lame joke, perhaps from relief that I wasn't about to get shit for the eyeing the bounty yesterday. I quickly compensated.

"I don't diagnose but I worked with mentally ill people off and on during my career. I know what the symptoms are, and most of us recognize someone who is floridly psychotic."

"This is always hard," she said. "Do I seem schizophrenic to you?"

"I hardly know you, Courtney. If you are, it's okay. I don't fear or stigmatize mental illness."

"I'm not mentally ill." Okay. What was she driving at? I glanced at the lizard. It seemed to be paying more attention.

"I sometimes appear to be talking to myself..."

"Lots of people do that. You should hear Kate go on after a bad day."

"Except, I am talking to someone." I stopped. Best to let her continue at her own pace.

"Your friend Tony is psychic, isn't he?"

"I prefer the term weirdo." This was going to go down in the bad conversation hall of fame. "Okay, I have come to believe that Tony has some insights."

"Why do you think Marie hired me for the navy?"

"You were joking about giant sea monsters, I assume because you're a fish scientist."

"We weren't joking, Chris."

"Do I need to revisit the schizophrenia theory?" She chuckled.

"You're breaking the tension," she said. "Thanks."

"Courtney, you seem like a cool person and you saved my life and the lives of my friends yesterday. I will always be grateful for that, even if you talk to dead people or something. Why don't you just..."

"I talk to dead people."

"Oh, I see." A silence followed. The lizard seemed to think it an opportune moment to disappear around the other side of the tree.

"There is a ghost on the beach who wants to speak to you." Was this a joke? Maybe Tony was somewhere taping this. Courtney seemed to guess what I was thinking.

"It's kind of serious. He says he knows you." There could only be one dead person on this beach who knew me.

"What's his name?"

"Doug Miles. He's over there, by that couple who can't decide if the water's too cold." The couple were stepping a few feet in and making faces.

"Come with me, and I'll be the medium." I rose to my feet and asked myself what was the worst that could happen.

We reached the water's edge where the water collapsed in asymmetrical waves, not strong enough to upset our balance. The couple had left, headed for the beach bar. Maybe if they got drunk enough they would take the plunge.

Courtney took my shoulders and positioned me so that I was facing her with my back to the water. "It's easier if it looks like I am talking to you. She glanced to the side and spoke: "I'm going to tell him." She looked back at me.

"Miles says he was murdered and he needs your help."

"What!" I was stunned and torn; was I being fucked with? On a short vacation a lot of strange stuff had happened; for all the sun and the cries of the birds, I was scared. But I found my tongue.

"What does this Miles guy look like?"

"He's tall, kind of handsome in a Marlborough man – oh, you're welcome – kind of way, short hair, weathered."

"That's what he used to look like; he didn't look like that last year."

"Ghosts can do shit like that…"

"Alright, I trust you Courtney, really, but you have to understand what this is like for me…" She shrugged and nodded. "Tell me exactly what he's saying."

She glanced to the side again and affected a gruff voice: "Allard, do you really think I want a goddam social worker from Scarborough solving my murder?"

"That sounds like him," I conceded. I looked in what I thought was the right direction and spoke: "What the hell happened?"

We stood in the shallow surf for what seemed a long time. Between the sun, and wind and emotional tension, I shivered a little. But the story was fascinating.

Between retirement and his wife's death Miles had been depressed and at loose ends. He hadn't been drinking; he emphasized that, but didn't know what to do with himself.

On a visit to Thunder Bay he had been importuned by a colleague he barely remembered from his days as a detective in Smiths Falls. They went to lunch and an offer had been made.

Money laundering was a growing problem in Northwestern Ontario. An organized group operated there successfully and the OPP intelligence unit wanted to find a way in.

Historically, smart young men learned how to go undercover and infiltrate gangs. But they didn't have time and came to the conclusion that an older retired cop might make the perfect plant.

Miles agreed. He was bored, sad and ready to direct his emotions in a constructive way.

His cover would be an older cop turned alcoholic. In public he would let himself go; drink, grow a beard, act like an ass.

The investigation was long and involved travel, but it eventually led to good intelligence that a cabal of criminals were funneling money through Northern Ontario into international banks in the Caribbean.

Not the Dominican Republic, but when Miles heard that two gang members had gone to a Dominican resort for a vacation he decided to follow.

"I had no idea what they looked like," he told Courtney, "and stupidly I didn't check in with my superiors. I just booked a vacation for myself. I thought I would keep my eyes open and see if I could find them.

"I tried to be a maximum ass with minimum alcohol but I needed a break. Just to be away for a bit. So I came down to the beach and the next thing I remember is standing to the side while you and Price pulled my body out of the water."

Miles' narrative was riveting and starting to feel weirdly normal. I looked at Courtney; this must be difficult for her.

"I'm okay," she said, anticipating my question.

"How do you know you were murdered?" I said to the empty air. "Maybe you slipped and bumped your head."

Courtney paused, looked at the space where Miles was supposed to be then back at me. "There was a witness."

Lucy re-enters the story

I paused myself and looked around. Despite this incredible story beach life went on as always. I realized that I would have some explaining to do if Tony, Brenda or Marie appeared.

"Okay, who is this witness? Another ghost?" Courtney nodded.

Of course it was.

"She's here now. Her name is Lucy. She has been on this beach for almost 200 years."

"Hello Lucy," I said with a glance to the side.

"Other side," Courtney said. I sighed.

"What did you see, Lucy?"

Courtney spoke: "She says… I'm not going to tell him that…, oh okay. She likes your ensemble."

"Thanks, the shirt is Sea Island cotton; my wife thought the pink was a bit much but…"

Courtney put a restraining hand on my shoulder after glancing to the other side. "Okay," she said. "You don't want to know what Miles is saying but he doesn't want to hear about your shirt." She looked the other way and listened.

"Lucy saw Miles from the other end of the beach. She saw someone hit him with a hammer and push him under the water until he stopped moving."

"Oh my God, did she see who did this? Can she describe him?"

"She was frightened. She watched from a distance." Courtney's face paled. "Really?" she said to the air. She turned back to me.

"She didn't get close to the killer but she saw whoever it was bury the weapon he used to kill Miles.

More problems

Moments later we were moving up the beach towards a sandy corner by the stairway, under the retaining wall. I pretended to talk to Courtney and we had to stop because a man and a woman were sitting in this corner, conspicuously not talking to each other.

"This is embarrassing," she whispered. "That's the guy Marie slept with the other night. He probably thinks I am here to call him out." The guy's wife opened her eyes and looked at Courtney with barely disguised suspicion. Now I was feeling embarrassed.

"Your buddy Miles is getting really pissed off. You should hear what he's saying about you."

"Tell him to... wait, I'll do it. Hold your goddam horses Miles. I can't hear you anyway so ha ha ha!"

Courtney risked a glance at the couple. The man looked up. His eyes widened with horror.

"*Is that her?*" the wife demanded. Courtney grabbed my arm and pulled me back towards the beach. I could hear the early stages of an argument escalating behind me.

"So?" I said.

"Lucy pointed to where the weapon was buried. It's under the chair where Marie's paramour is being lectured."

We were finally interrupted, but not by one of our friends. A senior Sunbeams staff, an older man in a light suit approached me.

"Mister Allard? I have been sent to bring you to the office of the hotel. Lieutenant Ortiz and Sergeant Panier are here to see you."

"Sure."

I felt a sudden chill come from nowhere. I turned to go.

"Oh Chrissy, aren't you going to say goodbye?" Courtney's tone had changed. I turned again. She approached me and planted a soft kiss on my lips. I could feel her breasts pressing against my chest. She leaned in and whispered in my ear.

"Sorry, this is the only way I could tell you. Miles just haunted you; for the time being he'll be everywhere you will be, see everything you see and hear everything you hear." She kissed me again, let go and smiled at the resort manager. He smiled back.

Too much was happening at once. Miles was going everywhere I was! Christ! I turned yet again and followed the manager up the stairs.

Ortiz and Panier

They sat a conference table, looking much the same as last year, though Panier had apparently been promoted. She gestured to a chair on the other side of the table. Three glasses of water were positioned symmetrically, two on one side and one on the other.

"*Vous avez de gros problèmes maintenant,*" Panier said. Then she smiled, and to my relief Ortiz did too. But he hadn't looked up from his notebook.

"Your wife becomes ill with cholera on her second day here and on the third day someone tries to blow up the boat you and your friends are taking to the island."

So they did believe us. He spoke calmly, with authority. "What do you think is happening?"

"I don't know." Except now I was beginning to have an idea. If Miles had been murdered... was the killer back? But why?

"We are going to interview everyone on that boat, and will stay in Samana for a few days," Ortiz continued. "This is a disturbing situation and we want to get to the bottom of it. And I want to know how you are involved." Something buzzed unnaturally in his phone. He picked it up.

"That's a new phone," he said with a frown. But he wasn't distracted long. The questions began.

I answered them honestly until he started to ask about Miles. And if he was like most cops he was pretty good at spotting lies.

The truth mostly worked; I told them about my Christmas enquiries and even my detective daughter visiting his son. The official sources had no opinion on his death; an accident as suspected.

The sins of omission were beginning to pile up. I now knew that Miles was working undercover and the murder weapon remained on the beach. What did I do with that?

If I dug the damn thing up how would it look? Never mind, I knew the answer; it would look like I put it there. Goddam it.

"Mister Allard?" Crap, I drifted out for a sec.

"Sorry, it's been a long week." They nodded.

"So you have nothing more to add about the death of Doug Miles."

"No." Ortiz's phone made another odd buzz. He looked again, his frustration showing.

"This was expensive," he said to no one in particular, still looking at the phone. He finally looked up and said, "Thank you Mister Allard. You will be on the property of the resort?"

"Yes, we booked for 14 days; we have almost a week left."

Kate on Chris's return to the room

I was waiting for him; feeling badly. Now, not so much. He walked in the door, acting like he had a lot to say but didn't know how to say it.

"You're in bed," he said, confused. "You're not sick again, are you?"

I slid the cover to one side and patted the bed beside me. "I'm feeling much better, darling. Why don't you come over here and make me feel better still." I then slid the cover right off of my naked body so my dim husband would get the point.

Chris turned away so fast he almost tripped.

"I'm glad you're feeling better, Kate. But are you sure now is the right time?"

"What on earth is the matter with you, Chris? Did something happen?"

"Yeah, a lot, can we maybe just get a drink and talk?"

"We're on vacation and I've been sick, and now I'm better and I'd like to…"

The alarm went off on clock. We both jumped.

"God, why does that keep happening?" Chris said.

"Maybe there's a ghost," I said, trying to make a joke. But Chris went white, looking ghostly himself.

"It happened to Ortiz too," he said. "Fucking Miles."

"Chris, I want to know all about this shit but right now I want to be alone. This is too weird." I pulled the cover back up.

"Sure, I'll go."

And just like that he walked out the door.

Fuck him.

Back in the lobby

The first thing I saw was Tony sitting alone at a table with a rum on ice. For some reason he had planted a small brightly coloured umbrella in the glass. I headed straight towards him, then saw Courtney and Marie entering from the stairway that led down to the beach.

I switched direction.

"Courtney," I grabbed her shoulders. "Tell him to go away!" She looked around. The bar was packed with the pre-dinner drinks crowd.

She looked around desperately and pulled me and Marie in close. Marie winked,

"*Tu es un peu mignon*," she said. But I was in no mood for levity.

"Tell Miles to fuck off and go back to the beach for the night," I said in a loud whisper. A light winked out over my head. "And while he's at it fuck off with the electric tricks." Courtney glanced to one side.

Her eyes widened. She looked aghast then looked like she was repressing a smile. She glanced again and said, "You want me to say what?"

"What?" I said. "What does he have to say for himself?"

"He says he's sorry he stopped you getting laid." Marie lost it. She laughed as if caught by hysteria. Everyone looked up. "And Mrs. Allard is still a fine looking woman."

"You tell him…" Courtney looked me in the eyes.

"I'm the intermediary. Tell me what you want." I took a breath, having said exactly that in hundreds of couples counselling sessions.

"Can you ask him?"

"Ask him yourself." Every therapist recognized this scenario. I looked over in the direction she looked.

"Miles, why don't you take a break for the night and go have a visit with, ah, Lucy."

"That's better, Chris... shut up, Marie, this is serious!" Marie looked like she was going to choke.

"So?" This was to Miles. After a delay she spoke to me: "He says you have to keep investigating his murder and let him haunt you during official investigative actions."

"Yeah, yeah. I'm committed now." I felt another chill. He was gone.

"C'mon, girlfriend, I'm hungry," Marie said. "*Désolé de ne pas t'être fait baiser, Chris.*" It was probably her accent but the tension broke within me and I laughed too.

"Go and have a good supper. Courtney, thank you. As a therapist, I know exactly how that felt." She smiled. Over her shoulder I could see Tony looking at us, curious as hell. "Oh, would it bother you much if I told Kate what you can do?"

"Will she believe you?" I shrugged. I liked these two women.

"Fifty-fifty," I said. "Go enjoy dinner."

Chris and Tony make plans

"Where's Brenda?" I said to Tony after a brief diversion to the bar. The barkeep put an umbrella in my drink too.

"She might have gone up to see Kate. Not sure; she said she would be back down for dinner. What the fuck is going on with you and Courtney? I saw her kiss you at the beach today."

"What! Tony, there's an explanation."

"Chill Chris, I know there is. I also watched a strange conversation that went on for almost thirty minutes on the beach. Not accusing you of anything, just want to help if I can."

"Courtney is a medium; she and I were talking to Miles' ghost, then he haunted me, then I saw Ortiz again and then Kate wanted to…Ugh…"

"That makes sense," Tony said.

"No it fucking doesn't, Tony! Don't tell me you believe me."

"Sure, I knew there was something different about Courtney. This lines up. There's something about a chair with the couple that are always arguing, and I think Courtney had to tell you something in secret."

"Anything else, smarty-pants?"

"Did you get a boner?"

I completely ignored *that* question and diverted myself with a sip from my drink. Tony was wearing a Bluejays hat. It didn't work for him.

"Tony… that hat doesn't work for you…" I started again. "Miles was murdered while working undercover and the murder weapon is buried on the beach."

"Shit, we have to dig it up and get it to… oh crap, how do we do that without looking like we planted it?" We both leaned back in our chairs. As if in tandem we both got sick of the umbrellas at the same time and put them in the ashtray on the table.

Stress and chaos can act on you in different ways. Tunnel vision – sometimes literal – is one possible outcome. But lateral thinking, outside the box is another. An idea had been floating around my unconscious mind.

"Tony, what if someone else found it, just by accident, while Ortiz and Panier are in town."

"How might that happen?"

I told him. To his credit, he only hesitated for a minute before commenting. "What if it doesn't work?"

"It will."

Sunday morning, poolside

"I'd rather go to the beach," Kate said.

"Aw c'mon, let's do the poolside thing today. The bar's better."

"Alright, if you want. I'll be closer to a ladies room if worse comes to worse."

It was her first day out and I knew she wanted to work her way back into the swing of things. Sitting around is fine if you are sick, but when you start to feel better it gets boring.

We were lucky, found comfortable seats and settled in. This was the hottest day so far and we slathered ourselves with sun screen and started with some available forms of internal lubrication. Kate cheated with a weak rum punch.

Tony and I had taken the evening to ourselves. It turned out that Brenda had decided to hang out with Kate so the timing was ideal. And it helped that we were lucky.

Tony found and purchased a box of small cigars, a Sunbeams tee shirt, a bottle of Breugal rum, and other sundries.

I found, with the help of the front desk, a computer with internet and access to a printer.

All this cost a bit of money but not more than buying a few souvenirs.

I needed time to create a document and suss out a decent translation on Google, hoping it wouldn't sound to strange to Dominican ears.

We met up again at nine, all items at the ready. Not many risks so far but the tricky part was coming up.

People who visit a heavily staffed all-inclusive resort behave in predictable ways; there are patterns to their movements. So we needed to make our next moves in a manner that conformed to those patterns.

We were going to end up looking guiltier than we were if caught; our actual activities would be quite benign.

We decided that intoxication would make a plausible cover, splitting up and appearing to be older men, a bit looped, and seeking space from the wives.

Tony had the toughest job.

I had to drop a few items off at different recognizable points; bottle of rum here, tee-shirt there. Tony had the list; he had to enter a small office where the recreation staff planned their day, leave it where it could be found and get out.

And he was caught.

"Amigo!" After a gentle hand on the shoulder, a befuddled Tony was led from the hut, carrying an open bottle of rum. He had deliberately set out to make a spectacle of himself, wearing a Prussian blue Hawaiian shirt with a straw fedora.

"I'm sure they think Canadian tourists are drunk and batshit anyway; why challenge expectations?" he said as we compared notes afterwards.

"Tony, in your case they'd be right." But I was grateful for his seedy past and associations. I heard a voice I recognized, saw someone I needed to see, and moved to complete the final piece of my plan.

So, by the pool on a Sunday morning, I waited. Most resorts have a cadre of young, attractive recreation staff, lurking by the pool to ensure noise trumps quiet and you never get too much into your paperback mystery.

I was counting on the idea that the activation people were handed a list of activities to execute every day or die trying.

This assumption paid off, though accompanied by an unexpected problem.

"Ladies and gentlemen, now we need all of your attention and participation in the next activity." Some keeners paid attention; most people didn't look up. "And today we have fabulous prizes!"

The slender and handsome young man reading this paused and turned to the similarly attractive woman to his side and said something; probably, "Who wrote this?"

But the mention of prizes picked up a few more heads, including, to my alarm, Kate.

"Today we are having a scavenger hunt, whoever wants to win a prize, come to the pool." Kate moved to rise. Nope, that couldn't happen.

"Stay with me, darling," I said. She frowned.

"Chris, this will be fun. Why don't you come with me? Maybe we'll win." I knew there would be a few moments as the staff tried to round up as many participants as possible."

"You'll be running around in the sun, probably sweating and butting elbows with civil servants from Brampton, all to win some shitty trinket." To my relief, she acceded to my request.

"Fine Chris, but we need to have some fun on this trip."

"I'm sure it's coming."

A young Dominican woman came over, took my hand and gave it a strong tug. "Don't you want to come with me?" she said with a pout and flirty smile.

"Too old and lazy," I said. Kate smiled.

"I missed my chance," I said.

A shadow fell across us both and we saw yet another attractive young woman – Canadian - in a yellow bikini standing over me, this time neither flirty nor friendly.

It took me a moment to recognize her as the woman who kept having loud public arguments with her boyfriend.

"Look at you," she said, "sitting with your wife." Her tone dripped with hostility. "After yesterday when you were making out with that hot girl – who fucks everyone – on the beach, right in front of me and my boyfriend." She turned to Kate.

"That skank fucked my boyfriend, and now she's fucking your husband." She paused and glared at both of us.

Kate looked up at her and slowing removed her sun shades. She fixed the woman with a cool glare. "Thank you. Your problem is with your boyfriend, not with us. Please go away."

The woman hesitated. Kate, in the right space, did not take shit from anyone. But then my wife recovered an old memory. Her voice softened. "I know how you feel, but your problem is with him."

The woman looked confused, then sad, then she turned and marched away, presumably to further berate her errant partner.

"Kate, it's not what you think!" I was near panic. "And it was Marie that slept with her boyfriend, not Courtney."

God, I walked right into it!

"So it was Courtney you were making out with?"

"Yes, but it's not what you think."

"You already said that, darling." I looked closer. After forty years of marriage you know when your wife is pissed. Kate looked more like she was trying to suppress a laugh. She changed the topic. "That poor girl is externalizing her internal distress. I know how it feels."

This was an uncomfortable topic for me, not helped by her appropriating clinical jargon. My cheating on her was an old wound, but one she would never forget.

People were running away from the pool with scavenger hunt clues in hand. The last one would dig and get a big surprise.

"Chris, I know you are up to something. I don't know what; maybe you will choose to share it with me. What I do know is that you haven't seduced a thirty-something hottie while I've been laid up with cholera."

I was being let off the hook by my insightful wife and took the implied tweak to my ego in stride. At least she wasn't going to ask me…

"*Did you get a boner?*"

Oh my God, she was someone else on vacation. She didn't wait for an answer but started to laugh, a little hysteria mixed in. I seized the opportunity to respond to a previous remark.

"Kate, if I'm right a few things should be revealed shortly. Then I will explain the rest."

We rested, read and I drank some more. In the distance, pelicans skimmed the waves, and local fishermen in narrow wooden boats returned from their morning rounds. I heard the hum of conversation, salsa music and people splashing in the pool.

Later, after many people had gone to lunch, the shouts began down at the beach. They were hard to hear but we saw guests running to the balustrade.

Now I could wander there myself, Kate – curious – behind me. In a minute, if they didn't block the stairs, I would go down.

I stood under the deck where they staged the shows every night, facing out on the beach. I saw Courtney among the crowd on the beach, standing at a ragged perimeter that had been formed around the corner table and chairs.

She had her hands over her mouth; looking shocked and hysterical; this, the woman who days before steered a boat with a ticking bomb into the bay then dived into the surf, seconds before detonation.

Dr. Snow wasn't much of an actor but she followed instructions perfectly.

I didn't see Miles and Lucy but I knew they were there, watching. I tried to imagine how Miles felt; which was hard since I couldn't see or hear him. But it must be a vindication.

Most people took the main stairway down to the beach. But another stairway ran down from the side. I took Kate that way. She looked worried but wanted to be with me.

We arrived and stood a few yards away. Hotel security staff had rushed to the scene. One spoke into a walkie-talkie. Another shouted instructions to wait staff.

I tried to get a look at the scene itself. A confused looking couple, maybe 50 something, stood answering questions.

"We had to do this, Chris." Courtney sidled up to me and whispered in my ear.

"You can kiss him again if you want," Kate said. Courtney flushed.

She looked at me: "Does everyone know?"

"Sorry," Kate said, not too remorseful. "What did they find?"

"The murder weapon," Courtney said. "It was a hammer with blood on it. The scavenger hunt led to a bottle with a note, saying: *Dig here.*

"Everyone was excited as that couple dug like a couple of poodles. Then they found the bag and started yelling. The recreation staff called security."

"So now shit hits the fan," I said. More people were coming to the beach and I saw a rope being tied around the site. More security people had appeared and the top of the stairs were being blocked.

"Funny how the scavenger hunt led right here, Chris." Kate stared at me.

"Yeah funny that." I wanted to brag. But I was too scared. Tony had wisely avoided the whole drama; and hopefully remained in his room with Brenda.

This was going to get weird quickly. Courtney spoke again.

"A Canadian buried that hammer," she said.

"What! How do you know that?" Courtney tilted her head toward the throng.

"They found it in a Shoppers Drug Mart bag."

Courtney

Those two might be older but they were smart as hell. Kate was putting two and two together at a furious pace, and Chris had set the whole thing up. I barely understood what was going on but somehow it was all mapped out in his head.

She didn't seem too mad that I had kissed him so I decided not to feel more embarrassed than I already did.

It was more embarrassing because, even though I pounced on him and it wasn't his fault, he had reflexively... *responded*.

He's a married old guy but I haven't felt that in a long time, and kind of liked it. Add to that Marie, happily banging away with guys in the room and...

Lucy and Miles stood by, staring in a way that only ghosts could. Time to move on.

Miles didn't seem like the emotional sort but I saw sadness in his eyes. The appearance of the hammer brought home the reality of the murder.

Shoppers Drug Mart, the retail pharmacy chain, is a Canadian phenomenon; ubiquitous in certain markets. Not likely anyone but a Canadian would have access to one of their bags.

I glanced backwards to check on the two ghosts.

"They look lost, don't they?"

"Not now Marie." I responded to the accent then realized that this was the wrong voice. I wheeled back and found myself facing a striking, well dressed black woman. She smiled.

"You see them, don't you?" the woman said. I stood speechless.

"Who are you?" I said.

"I am Sergeant Panier of the Dominican National Police. And you?"

"Courtney Snow, consultant to the Royal Canadian Navy."

The woman smiled. "You should see your face, *chere*. Do not worry, but we need to talk."

Shit hits the fan

Lieutenant Ortiz had appeared at the site, asked a few questions, and then allowed a security guard to point at me. He began to walk towards us.

He then escorted us to a piece of beach cordoned off from the rest. He opened his mouth as if he had something to say then closed it and started over again.

"What is Shoppers Drug Mart?"

"A chain of Pharmacies; they fill prescriptions and sell consumer items."

"I see. Canadian?"

"Yes."

"You can collect points," Kate added for some reason.

"And the Allard family shops there?" he asked.

"In our part of the world almost everyone shops there from time to time." He sighed. I didn't find this hard to understand from his point of view but I was nervous about how he might interpret the hammer's appearance.

"You understand police officers look on coincidence with grave suspicion," he said. I nodded. "And many questions are raised by the appearance of a bloody hammer on this of all weeks." Now he seemed to be more thinking out loud than asking questions.

A security officer turned towards us, perhaps to share something with Ortiz, thought better of it and turned away.

"So I ask myself. Why does this social worker from a place called Scarborough appear whenever something bad happens at this resort in my country?" He looked up at Kate and me. We said nothing.

"And indeed this has happened in his own country; appearing in Sioux Lookout in the 1990s during three murder investigations; even… being temporarily arrested for one of the murders; a woman with who he had previously been a lover…"

Kate flushed to the roots of her hair but remained silent. My blood pressure was rising but Ortiz raised a conciliatory hand.

"And yet, far from being ruined by disgrace, he rises from the ashes and solves the murders. Even today his daughter is a respected detective in Sioux Lookout. Senor Allard, what do you propose I do with this information?"

"I suppose you could hire me." Kate would have hit me if she could but remained still and stiff. I would hear about this later. Instead I heard the relentless waves and hum of voices on the beach.

"No, I will not hire you," he said, betraying no hint of either anger or amusement. "But I will ask you for cooperation should it be required."

He looked at me again; this was a question in the form of a statement.

"Yes, of course. What happens now?"

"The hammer is going straight to the forensic laboratory in Santiago and we have communicated with the Ontario Provincial Police. Given the appearance of the hammer, the bag from Canada and the death of a former Canadian police officer they are sending a task force immediately.

"Do you have any plans to leave the resort?" I shook my head. "I will be in touch." He turned and started walking through the sand to the crime scene. Then he stopped and turned back.

"Mister Allard, can we agree that if you have something to communicate with me you do so directly, and not in the form of a stunt?"

"Sure, Lieutenant, I can do that."

He left and I glanced around. Still no sign of Tony and Brenda. But I saw Courtney and Sergeant Panier having an animated conversation at the edge of the surf.

"We need to go back to the room and talk," Kate said. God, today everyone had to talk.

Courtney and Sergeant Panier talk

I recognized the body language at once, as she twisted to face the ghosts and appear to be talking with me. Like me, she had been doing this her whole life. She spoke first.

"Good to meet you, Mister Miles. I am Sergeant Panier of the Dominican National Police."

"Nice to meet you, Sergeant, and good to know there's a real cop on my murder, not just a social worker from Scarborough."

"Chris went to great lengths to get that hammer exposed," I said, feeling a need to defend him. "Sorry, but he's doing his best."

"It does appear that might be the murder weapon," Panier admitted. "We'll know more once it reaches the lab. I think you will be pleased to know the Ontario Provincial Police are sending a task force." Miles smiled.

"And you are?" The question was addressed to Lucy, who just stared.

"Lucy Jones," I said. Her eyes filled with tears and she spoke to Sergeant Panier.

"You are the police detective? A negro woman?"

Panier smiled warmly. "How long have you been here, Miss Jones?"

"Almost 200 years. I was a slave…. Miss Jones? No one has *ever* called me Miss Jones."

"On behalf of the Dominican National Police, I want to thank you for your contribution to this case."

"You are welcome," Lucy said. "Do you notice she says "sorry" too much?" She tilted her head towards me.

"Yes," Panier noted, "She is Canadian; they can be like that."

"No one has said sorry to me," Miles observed, "and judging from that Shoppers Drug Mart bag, the killer is Canadian." He wanted the conversation back on track. The Dominican detective started asking question.

Nothing was added to my previous conversation with the apparitions but at least Sergeant Panier heard it firsthand. She listened carefully and promised to pursue the investigation vigorously.

A constable approached us; Panier provided instructions and sent him on his way.

"Did you just give that man an order?" Lucy asked her. She was fascinated by the detective.

"He is my subordinate," she said. She was back to business. "Anything else?"

Miles had something left to say and seemed to have trouble saying it. "Allard is a big pain in the ass but don't shut him out of your investigation, he is liable to solve it before anyone else." Panier nodded and we left.

"Does Lieutenant Ortiz know you can talk to ghosts?" I asked.

"We do not discuss it. But he understands that I come up with information that no one else can. He does not push me to explain how. And your Commander Lesage, she is aware?"

"Yeah, that's why they recruited me." We arrived at the scene.

"Well, I must go," Panier said. "Please keep yourself available." And so I left.

Couples talk

I had been embarrassed by the incident of the hug on the beach with Courtney and hope that she hadn't been mad that my body suddenly decided it was 18 again.

But whatever happened played on Kate's psych and she jumped my bones the minute we returned to the room.

Later, we realized we were famished and agreed to head down to the buffet for lunch. While Kate was in the shower, the phone rang.

"Chris, did it work? I'm dying here; we came right back to the room after breakfast and laid low; I was so fucking tempted to check…"

"It worked perfectly, Tony. They found a hammer with blood on it!"

"Wow!"

"You guys hungry? Why don't we meet for lunch in a few minutes?"

So we all gathered in the buffet, ordered drinks and filled our plates. The place buzzed with talk as people from all over the world tried to make sense of the police presence.

All anyone seemed to know was that there was some kind of blunt instrument and a Canadian bag.

"So the ghost thing worked." Tony said, after swallowing some beer and waving a chicken leg.

"What?" Kate and Brenda spoke at the same time.

"The ghosts knew where the murder weapon was. Courtney can talk to them. That's why we set up the scavenger hunt and Courtney gave Chris the tongue job."

Kate had put most of this together, though not the ghost part. Brenda looked flabbergasted. Like most women, she had her priorities:

"What tongue job?" she said.

"What ghosts?" Kate said. She had figured out the scavenger hunt, knew nothing about ghosts and was anxious to change the channel from my necking with Courtney.

"I'm going to fucking kill you some day, Tony," I said. "But we owe the girls an explanation." So I proceeded to put them in the picture.

It was quite a story. Brenda didn't find the ghost thing as amazing as Kate but maybe being married to Tony took the edge off your capacity for surprise.

"Miles was in our room?" Kate said.

"Just that once." I didn't want her thinking he was present during today's lovemaking.

This was a lot to process and we compensated by going for dessert and drinking some more. Tony, eating vanilla pudding cake, broke the silence.

"I saw some shady tables on the far side of the spa. Brenda has cards in her purse; who's up for euchre?"

And thus passed the most normal, and as it turned out, the only normal day of our vacation. Two older couples sipping drinks, playing cards and stuffing their faces.

Later, after the "Caribbean Nights" show, we went our separate ways, and on to bed.

Disturbance in the night

Loud knocking.

I fumbled for the clock. Three am. In a deep slumber, I tried to bring myself to the surface and get to the door. After pulling on a pair of shorts I responded.

Two burly security officers from Sunbeams stood at the door. One of them addressed me: "Mister Allard, Lieutenant Ortiz wishes to speak with you right away." I was trying to clear away the fog.

"What is it, Chris?" Kate sat up in bed, holding the blanket to her chest. She sounded tired and nervous. I was pulling on a shirt. The men waited outside the door."

"I have no idea, Kate. I'll see what Ortiz wants."

"At this hour?"

"I know, it can't be anything good, can it?"

The men looked grim as I followed them down the hall and down the steps. As consciousness returned my nerves began to act up.

I was escorted out the back entrance and we descended to the beach.

A group of people were clustered in the distance. Strobe lights had been arranged around a site about 10 feet up from the water at the far end of the beach.

Sergeant Panier approached the men and me and held up a hand to stop. She spoke tersely to the two security officers who turned back to the resort.

"You will wait here for the Lieutenant," she said. She turned and left, leaving me standing alone in the dark. I felt a sharp chill that caused my body to shudder. The night was warm; was this shock or fucking Miles haunting me again?

When she appeared again, with Ortiz, he looked grimmer than the security guards. She gave me an odd glance before he spoke:

"Where were you tonight?"

"We watched the show with our friends then went back to our room for bed."

"And that is all?" I nodded. He turned to Panier and gave her instructions in Spanish.

"Sergeant Panier will confirm this later with your wife but…" his visage softened, "I believe you."

"I don't understand," I said, "what's going on."

"Come with me. Are you … the word…squeamish?" I didn't answer but the thought bubble over my head said, "*Oh fuck.*"

It was worse than I feared. The police circle surrounded a blanket, taken from one of the rooms, covering a body. A constable looked at Ortiz who provided a quick uptick of his head.

He pulled the blanket right off. Half naked, clothes torn, she was barely recognizable, though enough of her face remained for me to identify her. And people were looking at me. I had to say something.

"She was on the boat that nearly blew up. She was scared and Commander LeSage had to throw her in the water to save her." Ortiz made another gesture and the blanket went back on.

"I think she was maybe 16 or 17," I said, unnecessarily. One of the strobe lights blew out and Panier automatically looked at me. That gave her away. I glared right back.

Grabbing her hand I dragged her away. Every Dominican officer on the beach reacted. Guns were drawn. I was furious. It had been a long fucking week and I was at the end of my tether.

She looked over my shoulder and waved the other officers away. She then looked at me.

"Chrees," she said, sounding much like my mother, *"Je ne vais pas te faire mal. Dis-moi ce que vous pensez.'*

Vous voyez les fantômes, n'est-ce pas?

She put an arm on my shoulder and all the guns were put away. She laughed and everyone relaxed.

"Yes, I see the ghosts." I nodded. *"Chris, la fille a été violée."*

At that point, I lost whatever purchase I had on sanity. Rage flooded me in a hot wave.

"Miles what the fuck happened? I know you're here." I turned at random, yelling, "Miles *where the fuck are you?* Did you see this?"

"He's crying. He can't talk right now." That stopped me. Tears filled my eyes.

"Sorry, man."

"He saw it at a distance. He ran; he wanted to stop it but she was dead when he arrived. There were two people… he can't identify them. One had a cell phone in a pocket; Miles says he blew it up but by then it was over."

"Lucy?"

"She's falling apart. I can see her curled up at a far corner of the beach."

I remembered myself, finally.

"This is hard on you, isn't it?"

"Tu penses?" She smiled sadly. "I like you, Chrees. I am going to give you a good slap. It will calm down my colleagues. Then we will go back. *Bon?*

"Oui."

Back at the circle, she reported to Ortiz who looked at looked at me a few times, while I rubbed my face. Did he know about the ghost thing?

Shards of orange light appeared in the distance. Ortiz approached me.

"Senor Allard, we need to ask you a favor."

"Anything."

"The girl's name was Sabrina Maxwell. She was here with her mother." He organized his words. Something flashed in his eyes and I knew he had a daughter or daughters. "The mother is extremely distressed, I need someone to talk to her."

Brenda has a job to do

"I'm going to have to sedate her," the doctor said. He introduced himself as Dr. Fernando but he sounded like he'd just arrived from the San Fernando Valley. He continued:

"She is probably in a state of acute stress; I don't want her re-traumatized Ms. Price." He was clearly worried about the woman.

"I know what I'm doing," I said. "And she's going to be traumatized no matter what we do."

Chris and half the Dominican National Police had arrived at the door at 5 am. Tony and I were still in a deep sleep. I answered the door.

He had a disturbing story to tell. A teenager – she'd been on the boat before it blew up – had been raped and murdered.

This came at us suddenly; I saw a shadow fall over Tony but I had to control…the blackness in me. I held my hand out in front of me, to check it and calm down.

"Brenda," Chris said. "This woman is in a bad way. We thought a woman from home might be able to reach her. We need to know what happened and we need to know it now."

Tony had his cane in his hand, which had turned white. I knew he was thinking about whoever did such a thing and what he wanted to do to him... I wanted to... but I couldn't go there.

I briefly felt resentment then remembered what I was brought into this world to do.

Dr. Fernando ushered me into the bedroom. I vaguely remembered the daughter; pretty with mouse coloured hair, feisty and annoying.

Now I needed to be a social worker; a reflex, a calling and a commitment.

"This is Carrie Maxwell," the doctor said softly, then stepped back. She sat mute, white faced; one hand clutching a face towel.

"Hi Carrie," I said, "I'm Brenda. Where are you from?"

"Napanee," she said.

"Oh, I'm from Kingston," I said. "This is the worst night of your life but I need to talk to you."

She was maybe 50, a bit plump and wrapped in the first dress she found after the police came. She had poured a drink but maybe just for an out if she needed it. It sat untouched.

Napanee was an agricultural and working class town, just to the west of Kingston.

"Brina said someone asked her to go for a drink," she paused. "It made her feel grown up and on vacation." I nodded. Some people are traumatically open and some are closed.

She was going to tell me everything.

"I thought it was safe, there's lots of security, so I said go ahead, but be careful. I said be careful."

"Who asked her?" I tried to keep my tone casual.

"She could be very annoying, you know. Teenagers, well, they can just…" I put a hand on her forearm.

My job was to get the person or persons who did this. She couldn't fall to pieces just yet. Carrie took a breath. She glanced at her drink but decided to continue talking.

"She didn't say who it was. I just thought it was a boy." Now she realized the potential falsity of her assumption and I had to touch her again.

"When did you last see her?"

"About 10; I thought it was late for her to go out. That's late, isn't it?"

"Yes, it is. When my daughter was 16 I worried when she was out." My voice was soft; I was trying to project loving mother onto someone who desperately needed one.

"How do I tell her father? He loves her but he has a new wife and we don't get along." She was holding on by a thread; I could hear the doctor approaching.

"Mrs. Price…" I was out of time. I held up a hand.

"Carrie, how did she get the call, from the boy?"

"On her cell phone."

"Is it with her?"

"Yes, I think so."

"Can you give me the number? Then I have to go and if it's okay I want to tell the police what you told me."

"Yes... okay, tell them." She recited a number with a 613 area code.

"I will come back and see you, and visit when we're back in Canada. Now you let Dr. Fernando help you."

"Thank you, Brenda." She sounded waifish and childlike. My heart was breaking but I had a job to do. I had to speak to the cops.

A sombre breakfast, Kate

"When do the Canadian cops get here?" Tony asked.

"Chris, you talked to Roxy, what did she say?"

"They had to round up a team; two senior detectives and a translator. I called her last night and she said shit has really hit the fan. Wait until they find out what happened last night."

"I think we will see them today at some point."

Everyone was tired and discouraged. We all felt our age. Chris had returned to the room pale and exhausted, and then cried again.

Brenda looked every year of her age; on vacation and she had to go all social worker and interview the mother of a murdered teen.

She had been given the girls' cell number to convey to the police but that phone was missing, probably underwater.

Tony, how do I put this? He had seen more murder and mayhem in his life than the rest of us. He had tried to put it behind him, move to Kingston and now this.

I had the impression that he wouldn't be happy until he had killed the person who did this himself.

I felt useless, like they all had something to contribute but not me; my contribution was to get sick. Ugh.

We, and probably most of the tourists, knew that a murder had been committed but life went on, as if nothing had happened at all. We had signed on for two weeks in paradise but there were people coming and going to the resort every day.

It was clear that Ortiz and his team were good at working behind the scenes. They would try to determine where everyone was last night, if anyone had left the resort; basic police work.

They would not want an uproar but it was likely only hours before this story made the news almost everywhere.

Busloads of people came and went from resorts like this every day.

"Anybody seen Courtney?" Chris suddenly asked. I stiffened then asked myself why. This wasn't something to overthink. I was a bit jealous of the hot icthy… whatever she was.

"Someone - that Sergeant - talked to the ghosts last night, right?" Tony said. "They didn't know much."

This whole vacation was horrible – and weird.

"I just think she should be brought up to speed. She's been a big help so far. Miles is falling to fucking pieces – and he's dead! And it looks like Lucy is traumatized out of her fucking mind."

"Wait till you see Courtney, Chris." I said. "She'll find out soon enough. And you're cursing a lot." As soon as I said that, I knew what was coming. It was a good thing really, and always changed the mood.

Chris had a soft and melodic voice; it helped make him a good therapist and a brilliant hypnotist. But Tony had a clipped, deep Scarborough accent that emerged in a staccato baritone. Chris could imitate it, pitch perfect, every time.

*"It's that fucking fuck, Tony fucking Price. Can't hang around that nutwipe; can **someone** find me a fucking vodka…"*

Brenda laughed so hard coffee came up her nose.

"You're making me wet, Chris," she said, innuendo intended.

Tony was choking on his mimosa; for a minute we thought he might pass out.

And that is how the OPP delegation found us.

The new kids in town

"Are you, Mister Allard?" said a trim man in a light grey suit.

"Yes."

"I'm Inspector Ambrose Zhang with the Ontario Provincial Police."

He had noticed the obvious, that we were all batshit hysterical. I couldn't stop laughing.

"Sorry Inspector, we're pretty screwed up right now; long night and everything is seriously fucked. All of us have almost been killed this week and we've been triggered by that poor Maxwell girl."

Zhang glanced at the four sixty-somethings with flakey clothes and half drank Mimosas.

"I need you to come with me, sir. We're going to see Lieutenant Ortiz."

"Sure, you going to introduce me to your friend?" He smiled, just a bit, and turned to the shortish man with a tight goatee beside him.

"This is staff Sergeant Clark Piper. He is part of this investigation." Piper nodded.

"Alrightly, let's go then."

"Are you drunk, Mister Allard?" He put it in a way that didn't sound particularly hostile.

"One Mimosa. I'm good." I shuddered so hard I nearly fell over. Fucking Miles had to stick his nose in and haunt me.

My purchase on sanity was slipping by the minute. I glanced at Kate, she had never looked as worried. She took a sip of her drink. I was cut off.

"Chris, you're going to be okay, breathe," she said. Kate was right. The hysteria was only a gateway to a deeper level of calm; needed to go through it before the focus set it. Only then did I realize I'd forgotten to eat anything. Oh well.

"Allons, mes amis."

A difficult meeting

One more person from the OPP waited for us in the hotel board room. She was engrossed in conversation with Ortiz – in Spanish, though she stopped when I entered.

Piper introduced her. "Mister Allard, this is Gwen England; she's a consultant we use to aid in Spanish translation."

She looked at me, nodded curtly, and then returned to her notes. Her hair fell over her face, dark and thick. But I could tell she was a beauty. She looked up again, catching me looking over, and tapped a pencil on the desk.

"Welcome everyone," said Ortiz, "from the Ontario Provincial Police, and Mister Allard." He then looked at me.

"Mister Allard, there is no good reason for you to be here but given your proximity to certain situations and the reputation of your daughter, we have conceded that your psychological skills could be valuable to us."

"I'm happy to help. I understand this must be disturbing to everyone." I was trying to be diplomatic but Piper glared over at me and spoke.

"I need to be frank, Chris. I do object to your presence and have agreed to go along with this because Inspector Zhang insisted." Zhang glanced at his colleague. He didn't seem perturbed by the comment.

"I think we all want the same thing, do we not?" This was Panier speaking. "Lieutenant Ortiz and I have found Mister Allard's presence valuable."

I said nothing but Piper leaned back in his chair. Everyone had now been reminded who was in charge. Zhang looked at me and spoke.

"Chris, tell us about the Maxwell girl. We know the facts but I gather that you were with her in the boat that exploded and your colleague Brenda Price has spoken to the mom. Is there anything we should know about the psychological end of things?" My turn.

"She was like a lot of modern girls; headstrong and anxious at the same time. Lieutenant Commander Lesage had to literally throw her out of the boat to save her and Brenda had to drag her to shore.

"We are looking at an older man, some kind of predator with a practised skill set. And probably more than one individual."

"Why?" Ortiz asked.

"It seems obvious that whoever is behind all of this, the bomb, is getting a lot done quickly, arguably too much for one person. Planting cholera and setting bombs is not something the average guy can do.

"Sabrina was distant from her dad and she liked boys, but I find it impossible to believe that this was a simple liaison gone wrong. She was lured to the beach." Everyone was looking my way.

"My friends have a vague memory that someone slipped off the boat before it disembarked. But none of us got a good look. What if the girl did get a look? That would make her a threat.

"And they have to be here right now." The team was giving me a lot of rope.

"Why is that?"

"I think if it was someone among the Dominican staff they would have been spotted by now, or there would have been reports of employees leaving. If it was a Canadian, same thing, the staff would know. Almost everyone here arrived on a package tour."

"That sound like speculation to me," Piper said. He was leaning forward now. "I think we need to get back to straightforward policing." He was wearing an electronic watch of some sort that suddenly vibrated.

Miles was telling him to fuck off and shut up.

"Thank you, Mister Allard," said Ortiz. "I appreciate your comments and Sergeant Piper you are right about the policing. An Air Canada tour is departing today for Ottawa, we would greatly value the OPP's assistance in screening those who are leaving."

Shortly after, they booted me out and I was standing alone in the hallway. I glanced around so no one saw me. Satisfied, I spoke, "Okay Miles, you can go now. Why don't you go haunt that Piper guy?"

I felt a sudden chill. He was gone.

Courtney makes out

Jon was a big dude with a nice smile and an easy manner. He lay on the lounge chair next to me over his neatly laid towel with a thick paperback in hand. Putting it down, he announced to no one in particular that he was getting another beer. Then his attention focused on me.

"Would you like a beer while I'm up…?"

"Courtney, and the answer is, God yes." He laughed and departed.

When he returned with the beer he interpreted my acquiescence as an invite to chat, which in this case was true.

After exchanging pleasantries we came to the inevitable question, "What do you do?"

I told him I was an ichthyologist, leaving out anything about the navy or ghosts.

"I lead fishing charters on the East Coast," he said. "So here I am by the water for my vacation." He smiled but it seemed forced.

"By yourself?" I know that was artless but time was limited. He looked away.

"My wife flew back on a charter yesterday. She said she'd had enough; the marriage couldn't be saved and she was picking her boyfriend over me."

"Shouldn't you be crying in your beer?"

"My marriage has been over for a while and right now...I'm talking to you," he said, making eye contact. He reminded me of the young Robert Shaw. The implication was unmistakable. But he spoke again:

"I'm being way too forward," he said, stating the obvious. "I know you're here with that French girl; do you have a boyfriend or a husband? Oh, you're not..."

"I'm not gay and I have a boyfriend, but he's kind of dead, and a long way away." I had no idea what Nick would even think of this, but Jon was an actual man I could touch. How long had it been since I had..."

The shadow of that girls' death hung over all of us but if anything it increased my ardour. Listening to the relentless breakers and feeling the ocean breeze on my body, I was ready.

"I think the maid has been to my room; it's clean..."

Part of me wanted to go to my own room; it was less reckless and the idea of saying fuck you to Marie appealed, but I didn't want to be interrupted.

"Let's go."

Marie Lesage, the following morning, on the beach

I thought this vacation would be boring. Instead, everything has been livened up by death, mayhem and some good fucks. And the sun is shining this morning!

Maybe the biggest surprise; my girlfriend got laid last night! Good for her for her; she's needed a good screw since I met her.

She came in at 2 AM. I haven't seen a more satisfied creature since I took out a Cigarette boat full of pirates with a .50 Cal and looked in the mirror.

"Hey girlfriend, someone got lucky!" She actually looked around the room. "No, you, Courtney. Do I look stupid?"

"No, but I'd love to see how you look with a black eye, Marie." But she couldn't stay mad. In fact, she started to laugh. "God, it's been so long I've forgotten how good it felt."

"Pretty damn good," I agreed. "So, details?"

"Go fuck yourself, Commander Lesage. He was big, hunky and blonde. And that's all you are going to get.

"Did he fuck you doggy?"

"Shut up! And make sure I'm awake by 8. He says they've spotted an early Humpback whale; so he's rented a boat and meeting me on the beach at 10 to go out and see it."

"And you can hump on the way back." I thought that was hysterical but Courtney turned off the light and stopped talking.

So I set myself up early on a beach chair to get a look when Monsieur Hunky picked her up.

Courtney stood at the edge of the surf like a teenager on her first date, waiting for her beau. She was excited and had decked herself out in a cute blue sun dress.

I was not here to stay sober so I headed towards the bar stand, eye to the sea. Roderigo the bar guy pulled out the overproof rum he kept under the counter.

Tony Price was there, drinking a beer and leaning on his cane. He looked ridiculous in his purple tee-shirt, fedora and sunglasses.

"Where's your wife?"

"Sitting over there reading a book." He tilted his head towards an elderly woman lying on a chair. But he was looking at Courtney.

"She talking to dead people?" He said.

"Not this time. She's fucking some guy she met yesterday and he's coming to get her in a boat."

"Wouldn't it be easier to fuck him in a hotel room?"

"They're going out to look at some big fish or whale or something." He sighed.

As if on cue a white motorboat appeared on the surf, slowing as it rocked some of the breakers.

"He knows what he's doing," I said, looking closely. Without any words between us Tony and I were walking closer.

As advertised, he was hunky and blonde. Quickly out of the boat he was tilting the motor and dragging it to where Courtney could embark. He moved like an athlete. No wonder she was so happy.

Tony grabbed my hand and squeezed hard.

"Ouch."

"He's evil," he said. "Really evil."

"Sure your radar's not just picking up me?"

"He's way worse than you." I looked up sharply, then started to run.

It was almost worth seeing Courtney's face. If looks could kill.

"I want to see the whale too, girlfriend."

"Oh c'mon Marie."

"Who's your friend?" the handsome man said.

"Marie, this is Jon. Jon, Marie."

"She's welcome to join us." Now Courtney sighed.

"Sure."

"Wait for me! I like fish!" Tony was right behind me, staggering through the shallow water, looking like he was going to topple any moment.

The man – Jon – laughed. "Alright, all aboard! Setting sail for Samana Bay."

Kate, early afternoon

Chris and I were sitting in the corner of the lobby drinking coffee when Ortiz, Zhang and Piper came striding through. Piper stopped and shouted at Chris: "Allard, we need you now."

He shivered convulsively. I looked at Piper, then back at my husband.

"Chris, you okay? You're not sick are you?"

"No, just some Miles-itis. I have to go." I didn't like any of this.

"Fine, I'll go find Tony and Brenda. Be careful."

I was mad but what could I do?

Chris left and I started down the balustrade to the beach.

I found Brenda sitting up in her chair, staring out to sea.

"Where's Tony?"

"A boat came to shore to pick up those navy girls and Tony decided to walk out the water and get in with them."

"He didn't tell you?"

"No, he just got in." I could see her hands tightly gripping and shaking a corner of a yellow beach towel.

"Tony's impulsive, right?" She shook her head and leaned back.

"Yeah, Tony's impulsive."

The corner of the towel came away with a ripping sound. We both looked at the severed piece in her hand. She was really upset, or stronger than she looked.

A break in the case

Two managers stood stiff and silent outside the Board room. Led by Ortiz, we entered without knocking.

At the far end of the board table, a middle aged woman in a maid uniform was being interrogated by Sergeant Panier and Gwen England. I don't think anyone was being harsh but the sudden entry of four men frightened her.

"Gracias, Senora," Panier said finally. The woman nodded quickly and moved to stand. But Panier put a firm hand on her shoulder and gently turned her face until the two women made eye contact. She said one more word, eye to eye: *"Silencio."*

She stood back and the maid left as quickly as she could get through the door. Gwen stood up straight. She was even more striking now that I had a good look at her. She glanced at me then spoke:

"Two employees have now identified him as heading towards the beach on the night of the murder."

"Who?" I said. No one was listening.

"The managers are here, let's go," Ortiz said sharply.

"Where are we going?"

"There is a man staying here who may be a suspect. We are going to his room now."

"Do we need a warrant to search it or anything?" Ortiz sent a withering look my way.

Zhang shrugged and smiled. "Their country," he said. I followed the flow up the stairs and down a hall. A manager produced a key, slid it into the slot and stepped back.

Two Dominican officers appeared with shotguns. This was getting scary, really fast.

Ortiz and Piper went in first, the armed officers behind them. Moments later, Piper shouted to those of us who remained in the hall.

"It's clear, come in, but don't touch anything." Panier, who had disappeared, reappeared with a small brief case muscled into the front of the pack.

"I've got the print kit, boss," she said.

"He's not here, but the bed's slept in," Ortiz said. Panier was already at work with powder and brush. Ortiz barked orders at the two constables who turned tail and departed right away.

"I'm getting two sets of prints, sir." Panier shouted. Gwen looked up. Ortiz came striding over.

"Scan them, Panier, and send them to our database, Customs and Immigration, and Interpol. *Vámonos!*" I was beginning to see why Ortiz was in charge. He spoke and everyone listened.

Zhang turned to Piper, "Go with her. Grab your own scan of the prints and get them to our people, RCMP and CSIS."

In the end I was left in the room with Zhang, England, and one of the Dominican managers who appeared to be waiting for an excuse to leave. Gwen said a few words to the effect of "we'll lock up" and with a grateful nod he departed.

"Two sets of prints," I said to no one in particular. "Is he here with someone?" I suddenly felt stupid. "And who is he? Does he have a name?"

Zhang smiled. "Sorry Chris, you got caught up in the turmoil. The name on his passport is Ben Graves. Single so far as we know but we'll check both sets of prints. Right now everything is circumstantial; a few of the staff saw him in the wrong place at the wrong time."

I looked through the window. The view wasn't great this side of the hotel. We just looked out on a clump of palms. But maybe he wasn't here for the view.

Gwen looked perplexed.

"You okay?" I asked. She looked up again.

"Sure. You don't learn much about him from the room, do you?"

He'd left an open suitcase with generic tropical clothes and a few toiletries in the bathroom. Not much else.

"That seems a bit suspicious in itself doesn't it?" I leaned in and pulled out one of his shirts. It was huge. I checked the label.

"Wow, I didn't know they could put that many X's before the word "large". He's a big son of a bitch." Leaning in, I saw some fabric poking from under the bed. I reached and yanked out a silky blue bra.

The owner of this bra had clearly been generously provided by Mother Nature. Zhang and England looked over but their responses different.

Zhang flashed an amused smile then said, "Better leave that here in case we have to track down an accomplice."

Our translator didn't look amused at all. "I have to go and see if Piper needs any help," she said, then abruptly left the room. Zhang shrugged and we followed.

I felt uncomfortable and didn't know why. Sure, I hadn't slept but the impressions were coming in fast and furious. A bra's a bra right? No, something wasn't adding up and I was too fucked up to put it together.

A drink on the deck, Kate

Brenda had started wandering the beach; not so much looking lost as pensive. She was so full of contradictions; she could be wise and naïve at the same time; conscience stricken and ruthless.

But right now something was on her mind. I had come down for a walk but when I saw her standing staring out to sea, I thought it best to drag her up to the bar for a drink.

This seemed a good day for a bloody Caesar and they had enough Canadians in residence to stock Clamato juice; so we ordered two and found a seat. I broke the ice.

"I hope that wasn't too horrible this morning."

Brenda shrugged, as if interviewing a woman whose daughter had been found raped and murdered was all in a days' vacation.

She had followed me, but only now seemed to realize that I was present.

"Brenda, you don't have to…"

"Sorry Kate, sorry. No, sure it was horrible; I have a daughter - you have two; horrible as it gets. But I can go into work mode anywhere; that's not it." She shifted over in her seat to catch the shade. Her skin had always been fair; she didn't like direct sunlight.

"Tony got into a boat and went out to sea with those two navy girls and some guy the tall one – Courtney – found."

She had told me this before. It must be on her mind.

"I thought it was the short one sleeping with everybody." Brenda shrugged again and shifted a bit more.

"He didn't even say anything to me; just got in and left."

Again, the repetition. I sat and listened.

"Tony cheated on me every chance he could get for the first 20 years we went out together." I had guessed as much but never heard her state it out loud. I sat silently.

"I guess you know how that feels, Kate."

So this was Brenda angry. I had been with Chris a few months before he finally told her that he was going out with me. But we were young then, practically kids. She knew Chris's affair with a client left a wound that never went away, but I felt compelled to clarify.

"Chris only cheated once, with a client when he was director of the social work department at Metro General, but that was enough. He managed to lose his job and make the front page of the Toronto Star." The humiliation still cut.

"You ever cheat?" she asked. I shook my head.

"You?"

"No."

"We're such good girls," I said, with a soupcon of irony. Brenda lifted those deep blue eyes, and looked into mine.

"No, not really," she said. "Everyone has secrets, Kate. Cheating isn't the only bad thing you can do."

We heard some shouting; commotion in the lobby. Voices shouting in Spanish everywhere. Chris stood among everyone else, holding a piece of paper. He looked around, recognized us and headed over.

He arrived, smiled and we both glared.

"Wow, what have you guys been talking about?" He didn't wait for an answer. "Shove over, Kate, I have something to show you both."

After I had been relegated to the direct sun, Chris sat and put the paper face down on the table and began.

"Some of the staff saw a guy going down to the beach last night. So we went to his room with all the cops and they took fingerprints. And I found a bra."

"Of course you did. Police from two countries are chasing a desperate killer, and Chris Allard finds lingerie."

"It was big bra."

"God Chris, is that what you came here to tell us?" He was excited.

"No, the Dominicans and the OPP got hits on the prints. They belong to an assassin from Montreal named Alex Ventura. He's a bad dude, multiple alias'; he's killed a dozen people they know of; some with his bare hands.

"They think he's still in the hotel." Chris flipped the paper. "This is him. He's a big guy; in this photo he has dark hair, long hair and a beard. Brenda took in a quick breath. Then another.

"No, the beard's gone and he's blonde now, but that's him, for sure; I can tell. He's out on the bay," she said. "He's in a small boat with Tony and those navy girls."

More violence

I was on my feet seconds after Brenda's disclosure. I spotted Piper at the desk and passed on the news.

"Any idea where they were going?" he asked.

"No, according to my friend her husband just embarked on an impulse." I knew why. Tony would have spotted the evil and followed it. And this guy was evil.

Something I knew about Tony; he was brave as hell; nothing scared him.

"Okay, I'm going to get Ortiz; I don't know if they are coming back this way but…"

Someone shouted in Spanish from the top of the stairs. Sergeant Panier, Inspector Zhang and two cops sprinted by. We followed.

"Where's Gwen?" Piper yelled, looking around. "This is what we brought her for."

A crowd had formed on the beach. I paused and Brenda ran past me. Even in old age she was fast. I followed her down and pushed through people towards the surf.

A boat had landed. Brenda was at the edge of the fray so I took her hand and started saying, "Policia" to break through. A constable tried to stop us but Panier looked up and shouted at him to let us through.

My sandals got stuck in the sand, I stopped, plowed through and we stopped in shock; unprepared for the sight before us.

Courtney sat on a bench by the bow, wrapped in a blanket. Her face was turned inward as she quietly wept. Tony waved to Brenda. He looked as unperturbed as ever, though a jagged bleeding cut ran down the left side of his face from the bottom of the eye.

Marie was tending to the motor. She turned and grinned. At least one of her teeth had been knocked out.

As to Alex Ventura the only part recognizable were some strands of dyed blonde hair. The rest bore more resemblance to chopped meat. They had stuffed him between two seats.

"This guy might be dead; not sure," Marie stated with a slight lisp and the kind of emotion we reserve for ordering coffee.

Security staff helped them off the boat, leaving Ventura for paramedics. Two had already arrived but, ignoring the bloody lump in the boat, tended to Marie and Tony.

Brenda was already at his side. Sergeant Panier sat in the boat, an arm over Courtney's shoulder. I saw them both look up at the same time, at nothing in particular.

Miles was here too.

"So, we have found our killer?" Ortiz said. The question he asked was rhetorical. Probably we had, but still, too many unanswered questions. I addressed Zhang:

"I think we know who owns the blue bra." He nodded. "I don't think she had anything to do with this, though. I think Courtney just fell for a guy she liked."

"Maybe he found her," Zhang suggested. "This guy is a sociopathic predator; we've guessed he had a sideline preying on women and girls."

"We'll have to talk to Dr. Snow but I suspect you are right," Ortiz said. "I don't understand what happened to him though; he's in rough shape."

"I think he preyed on the wrong marks." I looked again at Tony and Marie and couldn't help think they'd just had the most fun of anyone on this crazy "vacation."

As they left, Courtney still sniffling, with Panier, Ortiz and Piper, Brenda sidled up beside me.

"They don't look too contrite," I said. Brenda smiled.

"That guy raped and murdered a young girl and Tony took out another monster. Believe me, he's got a song in his heart. He's going to be in a state tonight." The look on her face suggested this "state" might not be unwelcome.

Marie glanced over at the near corpse, cocked her hand and fingers like a gun and pulled the trigger.

I think her heart was singing too.

Kate finally made it through the crowd.

"What happened?" she said.

"Tony and Marie nearly killed the killer." The paramedics had turned their attention to the lump in the boat. It moved convulsively. So he was alive. They roughly bundled him onto a stretcher and moved to take him away.

"Christ do I need a drink," Tony said. He probably did, but first he would need to spend time with the cops.

"I'll get a couple of cold drinks and snuggle up to the girls while they give you the third degree." A good clinician has to master timing and in saying the douchiest thing I could think of managed to make almost everyone laugh.

Even Ortiz cracked a smile. He caught himself and added his own comment:

"Mister Allard, you *are* going back to Canada soon?"

"Yes."

"Good."

Later, in the piano bar

They didn't keep Tony too long. We all convened in a corner of the piano bar where, fortunately, no one had yet tried to abuse the ivories with popular tunes.

"I told them that after he confessed to killing the girl, and pulled out a gun to kill us, Marie and I beat the living shit out of him."

"You make that sound simple," I said. Tony had arranged to have an unopened bottle of Stoli brought to the table. He was clawing at the wrapping. It was one of those bottles with plastic spouts. You rarely see them in Canada.

"They tell me that Ventura cocksucker is a really bad guy."

"Is?" I said.

"Yeah, he'll live." He turned his attention back to the bottle. "What's the matter with this fucking thing?"

Kate was looking a little green. She was used to Tony and even liked him but I had a feelings she'd make an excuse and go to bed soon. Still, watching Tony fumble with an unfamiliar bottle was too much for her.

"Give me that damn bottle, Tony." Still looking closely he passed it across the table. Brenda chuckled.

"Tony's perfect day, almost ruined," she said.

"I knew he was a bad man and he knew I knew. But we played out the charade until we reached a small island and disembarked."

"Another island?" Kate said. She was looking down but also making progress with the bottle.

"It was just a sandbar with a few rocks, trees; about the size of the parking lot behind an elementary school. As soon as we disembarked he produced the pistol."

"Gotcha!" Kate had the bottle working and poured a stiff measure into a glass. Brenda reached into a bowl of ice and pulled out some cubes. Tony paused and continued, sure he was going to get the first drink.

"The worst thing was seeing Courtney's face. The shock. And I'm not sure that Marie believed me either until this happened. She swore and that's where he made his mistake. He turned the gun and I was closest.

"The mistake people make is stepping back."

"Is that what they call mansplaining?" Kate said. She handed the first drink to Brenda.

"Yup," Brenda said. She took a deep drink. Tony looked annoyed but if Kate was fond of Tony, I knew the feeling was reciprocated.

"I got him down. But he was strong, got a good shot into my face and right back on his feet. Then Marie waded in." The drink was now in my hands but I was too fascinated to interrupt the narrative.

"I don't know who trained her but she's fucking ninja. She knew exactly where and how to hit.

"Then he said, 'if any of you have a daughter she's next.'"

"Hoo boy," Brenda said. Tony looked over.

"He's lucky you weren't there," Tony said to his wife. Kate smiled but Brenda nodded. I had a feeling there was something more to that comment.

"So," Tony had his drink now, he took a pull, "I kind of went apeshit on him."

Tony was close to his daughter.

I understood but I also felt like I needed to comment: "Is all this bloodlust cathartic for us?"

"Probably," Kate said, surprising me a little. We understood that Brenda for all her librarian manners and innate sweetness, had a dark side.

But Kate, though sickened morally and physically by this week was further away from darkness psychologically, so more apt to notice its incursion.

"Now we have to find the other guy." That stopped everyone dead. All eyes shifted to me.

At once the other voices and sounds in the bar could be heard, including some drunk idiot trying to play Chopsticks on the piano.

"We agreed there was someone else. The ghosts saw two people." Okay, that was lame; so I continued on a more logical path. "We agreed that too much has happened for this to be the work of one man.

"From planting the cholera virus to setting the bomb; no, there was someone else."

"Maybe this guy will spill the beans," Tony suggested. "I'm guessing the Dominican authorities will be…persuasive, with someone who killed a cop and a young girl on their soil." I shook my head.

"I saw this guy's record. He is a very bad man and a pro. Even in a place like this he's going to keep his mouth shut no matter what they do to "persuade" him.

"On that note…" Kate interjected. "I'm wiped out now and I shouldn't drink more vodka." She looked at the empty glass in front of her with disingenuous regret. "Oh…"

Courtney Snow, eyes red from crying, had entered the bar and approaching our table.

Courtney talks to Chris

"So?" I started the conversation. She flashed a wan smile. I knew she had experienced an ordeal but no one was going to mistake her for a fragile person.

Everyone else had shuffled out. Brenda had put a warm hand on Courtney's shoulder after she asked to speak with me. Kate had dug a surreptitious finger into the back of my neck and Tony had called for more ice and clean glasses for the vodka he left behind with us.

"It's okay to talk to you?"

"Yes, of course." Courtney looked shame faced and seemed to be having difficulty making eye contact. She did look over at the vodka bottle, as if noticing it for the first time. She reached out and started to accumulate the makings of a stiff drink.

"My parents died in a car accident five years ago," she said. "And Marie is a great friend but counselling isn't her long suit." Drink ready, she took a long appreciative pull.

"It's okay," I said. "We go through crazy shit and we reach out for support. That's the way it's supposed to work."

"It's been a long time since I've had sex with a man; my special friend is a 200 year old ghost…"

"Who's not into sex?" This made her laugh.

"He's totally into sex; he just can't touch." She looked down at her drink. "If Nick could, Nick would."

"That's his name?"

"Yeah, he owned land and a farm in Kingston until he was murdered."

"Poor guy. Do you feel like you cheated on him?"

"No, no, I don't think he would have a problem; he understands."

I would have guessed that. I knew what this was about but Courtney needed to raise it when she was ready. Her hand was turning white around the glass. For a moment I was afraid she would break it. Here it comes, I thought.

"He raped a young girl and then I had sex with him the next night." Her words emerged, anguished and strangled.

I knew she wasn't quite done.

"And I liked it…"

Her chest started to heave. A few people noticed but I was locked in on her. In a "do what you want" world many have forgotten the power of the demon of guilt.

And, come to that, the emotional connection of sexual intercourse. The wrong thing to do here was contradict her emotional experience by saying nothing was her fault. The right thing to do was allow her to put it together herself.

"Do you hate me, right now?"

"No. Courtney, look at me for a sec." She raised her eyes.

"Did you know he raped Sabrina when you slept with him?"

"No, but maybe I should have."

"Courtney, you are a scientist. You are also brave as hell. Of course you feel shitty. What normal person wouldn't? I would ask you to be ruthless in facing the fact that you slept with the wrong guy *but you had no way of knowing that.* That is simply a fact." I kept going:

"That has to be processed. It will take some time."

I had a weird thought; not one that usually came up in counselling.

"She's not still down there is she?" Courtney shook her head. She poured more vodka into her glass.

"No, Miles says she went into the light almost right away."

That was a relief.

"You know my history." Statement not a question. We all knew the miracle that is Google. She nodded.

"It happened at a bad time in my life but I still knew what I was doing. Sleeping with a client is the biggest mistake you can make. There are no shades of grey.

"I know you can intellectually see the difference but think about it; in time you will see that I did something much worse than you."

"That's supposed to make me feel better?"

"No, but it is supposed to help your process."

"Okay."

There wasn't much more to say. Her disclosure was as much confession as anything else, with me cast as the priest. I was glad she trusted enough to say what was on her mind.

"So who's the other guy?" Courtney asked. I picked up my glass. Chopsticks guy had left and someone new was approaching the piano. Uh oh.

"That's the big question isn't it? I'm trying to look at this laterally and see if something pops up through my subconscious." An intoxicated youngish man slid onto the bench in front of the piano and started to play what I think was a Billy Joel tune. He hit a lot of flat notes.

"Thanks Chris," It was clearly time to go. Kate would want me back at the room and Courtney had said what she came to say. We got up to leave and exited the bar together.

An interlude with Bob Wong

Bob and I went back more than thirty years, to the time when he was head of Psychology, and I was head of Social Work at Metro General Hospital.

He now – and for many years - ran one of most successful corporate counselling practices in Toronto. When everyone else in my field abandoned me, he and Kate had decided to keep me.

Whether this was arrogance, affection, self-interest (I was the best therapist he'd ever hired) or a combination of all, he was someone I could count on.

He was a big man who loved living well, though this was much chastened by a heart attack a few years back.

So the following morning, after breakfast, I told Kate I was headed back to the room to give Bob a call. She knew what that meant.

"You really are trying to solve this."

"Of course I am. I may not end up punching someone out like Tony but I'm as motivated as anyone."

"As if you could punch anyone out. And Tony only lived to tell the tale because that psycho navy lady helped him out." This was Kate at her most exasperating.

"I do have a brain to use, Kate."

"Chris, you *do* have a brain so think about this. At this point someone very much wants to kill you. Don't make it easy for them."

"If the Dominicans catch him he won't be able to do anything. So let's make it easier for them."

"Is this what you therapists call grandiosity?"

"Yes." She made a show of throwing her hands in the air.

The OPP trio sat a few table over, eating their breakfast. All three had glanced over, offering variously a hand on the forehead (Piper), a withering look (England) and a chuckle (Zhang).

Shortly they would be starting real police work, and I was off to my room.

Bob liked people to think he was busy; deeply engaged in cases. In truth, he did what many successful leaders did best – hire people like me to do the work.

I didn't resent this, or his success; he paid me well and I enjoyed the clientele.

If a stranger rang up he might have feigned activity but he took my call from his 20th floor downtown suite right away.

"Chris, why the hell are you calling me while on vacation, and when are you coming back?"

"I love you too, Bob."

Since he had me on the line anyway, he might as well perform a small guilt trip. "George Foster the third has discovered fentanyl patches and his parents are freaking out."

"Will he come in?"

"I think so, for you."

"Okay, I should be back next week. Find a time and I'll see him. What a fucking mess." But this wasn't why I had called. "Bob…"

"Oh wait, you're in the Dominican aren't you? Please God this isn't about that cop that was murdered."

"Yup."

"Okay, and you want to tell me about it." He didn't wait for an answer but yelled to his secretary: "Sasha, bring me an expresso with two…no, one sugar."

"I'm glad you are looking after your health Bob."

"You did call me to solve this murder for you."

"No! When have you ever done that?"

"Every time."

"That is so not true. But if you have some time (ironic cough) I do want to run it by you." I could visualize him settling into his chair, much like a Cantonese Nero Wolfe. So I spilled the lot.

His first words after I finished were, predictable:

"Ghosts on the beach? How much you been drinking old friend?" But he didn't wait for an answer; attributing the subject to my eccentricities.

"Chris, for God's sake, get on a plane and bring Kate home today. Cholera? You should have brought her back a week ago. This is just irresponsible.

"And sorry, you're traveling with that alcoholic fruitcake Tony Price (no love lost there) and two lunatics who hunt monsters with the navy. Have you checked their credentials? The only people who sound sane are Zhang and Ortiz.

"Say something helpful, Bob." It was warm in the room today. I was hoping the maid wouldn't come in before we finished.

"And I am doing this for charity?"

"Drinks at the Royal York, in the Library Bar when I get back."

"Okay, fine. Chris, Kate's right as usual; you are in danger. You've established a legend as someone who solves murders so you are a threat to whoever the remaining killer is.

"But there's something else you've forgotten." He paused for dramatic effect; a trick every therapist understood. "The main threat you pose – the obvious threat is that you can ID the killer."

"No I can't."

"Sure you can, and so can Kate. You were both given the extra water; I am sure that both glasses contained cholera; meaning they wanted you both sick.

166

"Chris, we solved…"

"I solved…"

"Fine, you solved a couple of murders twenty years ago in Sioux Lookout. That hardly makes you Sherlock Holmes. Use your head; you saw the killers last year.

"Bob, I briefly saw this Alex Ventura guy but his face was unrecognizable. I did see a picture but I didn't recognize it, though in the picture he had a beard and different hair."

"The context may have been different. But I'd bet my last nickel…"

"Unlikely to come to that…" I glanced out the window. Some gulls were circling the waterfront.

"You know the killer and if you access your memory, you will remember who it is."

I waited a few moments.

"So that's it?"

"Did you want a name?"

"Okay, thanks… I guess."

"I'm free for those drinks next Thursday."

"Fine, if I'm still alive, I'll be there."

"Chris…"

"Yes Bob."

"Stay alive, I want one of their seventeen buck martinis."

Back to the beach

Kate was waiting for me. She had pulled two of the beach loungers together so we could chat.

The day had evolved from a foreboding early morning to a cloudless sky with sharp hot light competing with a cool breeze off the water.

We sat well back against the aged stone retaining wall separating us from the highway.

She even disappeared for a moment and came back with a couple of cold beers.

"Thank you darling," I said.

"Well, what did Bob say?" I told her.

"That's all?" She was disappointed.

"Honey, think about it. Maybe it hasn't been my genius as a detective that's put us in harm's way." She rolled her eyes. "We saw something last year; probably the killer or killers. We're witnesses."

Kate frowned.

"The other guy must be mad." I took a sip of my beer. Too light but awfully good in this weather. A small cluster of middle aged people standing a few yards ahead of us, laughed at a joke in German.

"Why, because, like Inspector Clouseau, you've evaded every attempt to kill you and your buddies. Tony and Marie beat this Ventura guy within an inch of his life. Of course he's mad. He probably wants to kill you more than ever."

"Us," I said, "he wants to kill us. Kate, do you even remember anyone we saw here last year? I think I remember the barman, and one of the maids looks familiar but that's it."

She shrugged. She had no idea.

"I remember a lot about that week; more than I would normally, because we found Miles' body, but that's about it. And you probably only remember a maid because you think she's hot."

That was probably true… no, maybe not. I probably recognized her because I had some kind of interaction with her; quick chat or a laugh of some kind.

"Hey, check out Piper and England," I said.

They had set up two chairs between us and the booze hut, grabbed some kind of drink and looked like they were going to go for a swim. He wore a pair of purple trunks and she had put on a sea green one piece suit. The breeze and the waves were gentle today but they weren't on vacation.

"I'm going to get us two more beers," I said. Ignoring the skepticism on my wifes face, I started to make my way through the sand, trying to avoid rocks and sticks and other deritus.

"Is this where my tax dollars go?" I said to the pair, hoping a jocular tone wouldn't make it offensive.

But my tonal efforts were wasted on Piper.

"It was a long night, Allard. We're meeting with the Dominicans in an hour, so we are trying to use a little cold water to wake ourselves, as if it's your business." He glanced at the drink. "This is mango juice," he said.

He hated the impulse to explain himself and it showed.

"I'm supposed to be on vacation," I said. "Anyway, I didn't mean to offend." My eyes were drawn to Gwen. Man, she was hot, and not from the sun. In one of those silent, almost subconscious responses, she drew a red beach wrap over her legs.

"Am I invited to the meeting?" I said.

"No." Piper said. "Your wife's looking over. Get her a drink and then go dunk your head in the ocean."

I spilled most of a beer on the way back and gallantly handed Kate the full one. She was still looking over at the cops.

"I saw you checking out the lady cop," she said. Enjoying the upper hand for a moment, she handed me an out, "she does have great legs."

"Yes, she does." I sighed and took the remaining sip of the beer. In a minute, I'd need to go for another one.

Friends at the bar

"Why not me? Tony said.

You must be joking," I said. "Tony, in some ways you are the best social worker ever, but hypnosis?"

We were surrounded by white upholstery, coral walls, the greens and Indian yellows of the palms, and pink walls. Kate and I had graduated from beer to margaritas. We held the large sweating glasses close.

I was the only one, based on the angle of the orb in the sky, sitting in direct sunlight. I was trying to figure a way to getting out of it.

The idea had come to me while we climbed the steps to the buffet.

If you have a lost memories there are things you can do to retrieve them. Associations can bring them back, as can the simple recounting that inevitably connects conscious thoughts.

But those things hadn't worked, and there was another alternative.

I had joined the Canadian Society for Clinical Hypnosis about 10 years back, and had also taken advanced courses with the American Society.

My mother had been skeptical but impressed by the rigor of modern practise. Angela, to my great pride, had joined me in hypnosis, and the Society.

This felt good to me. Roxy was the cop and the Cossack in the family; she shouldn't have been closer to me than her sister, but she was.

Angela had always been more reserved.

I knew enough to understand that she expressed her love and passion differently than her sister. Temperamentally she resembled Kate; I loved her so much, but rarely felt like I was reaching her.

She became a therapist – like me – and it took time for me to realize that she wanted the connection as much as I did. Hypnosis was something father and daughter could share.

So when it occurred to me that I could access the memory of the killer through hypnosis I briefly considered using Angela through Skype.

But even though I had hypnotized people on Skype before, I didn't trust the signal to hold for the subtleties of an induction at a distance.

So, in the bar, over drinks, I asked Brenda to hypnotize me.

"I can walk you through the whole thing," I said. I took a sip and looked at Kate and my friends. These were awesome Margaritas. Tony offered; he was a bright guy but I needed someone with a subtler state of mind.

Kate; well, she wasn't hypnotist material. She sat silently while I dragged another woman into an emotionally intimate place.

"I've never tried doing hypnosis…" Brenda said. There was no question of her doing it; she always rose to responsibility, but I could tell she was nervous. I was asking a lot.

"This isn't about accessing a traumatic memory; it will almost certainly be something trivial; a chance encounter or someone I saw in the bar." I shifted in towards Kate, to get more shade. She shoved back.

Regression hypnosis was like that; subjects associated into small things; remarks or events that seemed like nothing at all yet resonated with the unconscious mind.

"I will teach you a simple "going down" induction." Tony raised his eyebrows.

"Oh fuck off," I said to him. "Brenda, it's probably more accurate to say counting down, but truthfully, I will be hypnotizing myself. I will need you to walk me around the compound here.

"We will use language to associate me into sensory memories; easy peasy."

"Chris, you don't ask much from your friends, do you?" Kate said.

"I want to do it," Brenda said. "I want to help." Kate nodded. "Besides, you will all be there, right?" They nodded.

"Chris, you are going to push me right off my seat, do you want to change places," Kate said. The sun was cooling anyway, and sinking into the sea.

"Let's get some supper – its Mexican night – and meet at eight in our room."

Hypnosis by candlelight, Kate

He made a drama out it; and even made it entertaining. Clinical hypnotists swear up and down that their work is serious and not for diversion. Chris liked to say that a hypnotist who performed on stage was no different than a massage therapist who provided hand jobs.

But that's more self-deception; they are all big fucking hams who love the excitement.

So he dimmed the lamp, lit a candle and reminded us of our larger purpose. Then he sat in a comfortable chair with Brenda just off centre facing him, and Tony and me sitting behind her, on the bed.

He spent an hour with Brenda giving a miniature introductory course on inductions and hypnotic language. He told her that she would be the tour guide; he would do the work but she could guide and steer him with the hypnotic language.

Chris swears that, back in the day, he never slept with Brenda. But I had always suspected some kind of intimacy. Now I was realizing the relationship between the hypnotist and subject, while not sexual, was intimate in other ways.

Chris was settling into the chair and Brenda was checking some notes she had made, when we heard a sudden crack. Everyone looked up.

"Sorry guys," Tony said, waving his hand. "Just opening a beer. I'll be quiet now." I giggled and Brenda began.

She was pretty good. She had the voice for hypnosis; soothing and calm. For much of duration, I think Tony and I were in a mild trance as well.

A few times she stumbled over words but it really didn't matter; she called attention to his sensory experience, rooted him in the present, challenged his sensory imagination and walked him down a hill on a warm and sunny day…

"Nine, down, down, deeper…

"More relaxed, and eight, deeper still…"

Until finally he stood at the bottom of the hill, *"feeling safe comfortable and relaxed…"*

Chris had struggled whether to have her do all the talking, to have him talk or use autonomic finger signals.

In the end he had decided on the signals; maintaining that it would keep him in a deeper trance and able to access memories.

So Brenda was the tour guide; taking him back through the mist of time one year, and into that experience; at the resort, on the beach, in the buffet and restaurants, the room…

Christ, the room! Would he remember… us? A smile flickered across his face, while mine turned read. A barely perceptible chuckle got choked off in Tony's throat. I wanted to elbow him but resisted the urge.

We watched him closely in the candlelight. Brenda was going sequentially through the experience. From the room, we moved back to the beach…

Chris stiffened and he quickly sucked in a breath…

Brenda was on it.

"Do you see something?" His right index finger jerked up; the signal for yes.

"Are you seeing the body in the surf?" Again, the right finger.

"Do you want to go closer?" I could hear the faint sounds of merengue music drifting up from the poolside. My eyes never left him though, as his left index finger moved, the signal for no."

Chris warned us that an abreaction – associating into a traumatic memory – might occur at some point but Brenda was ready.

"Now moving back… back, back, just left me know when the emotions just fade…" His right finger moved. "Very good… now moving ahead in time…"

She steered Chris through the arrival of the police and the night up to breakfast the next morning. He changed again. He started to move his head sharply around.

The other warning he had delivered had to do with trusting the unconscious mind; if it tried to communicate something, you listened.

"Do you see something?" The right finger.

"Do you want to leave?" Left finger.

"Then take this moment in that time and learn everything you can about what you see, and just let me know when you have seen enough…"

After a bit he made the signal and she finished out the week without further incident.

She then counted again; up this time, to five, bringing Chris back to the room and allowing him to slowly open his eyes.

Tony cleared his throat as if to speak but Brendas hand shot behind her onto his knee to stop him. They read each other's cues.

Chris needed some time to come out of trance, and Brenda was being possessive about her client. He took some deep breaths and said, "Thank you, Brenda, you were awsome." I shot her a glance. Both of them looked like they'd just finishing fucking.

Even Tony had a lopsided smile, suggesting that the same thing crossed his mind. Unlike me, he seemed to enjoy the idea.

"Are you okay, Chris?" I said. It was time to remind everyone that he had a wife in the room.

"Yes, thanks. That was really something." He sighed. The music outside had grown louder. It reminded us that this weirdest of experiences was supposed to be a vacation.

"I've had worse vacations," Tony said, as if reading everyone's mind. Brenda moved her chair so she could look at her husband.

"Sioux Lookout," he said, as if that was self-explanatory. Kate and I looked at each other and nodded. For some of us it was.

"I have to go there some day and see for myself," Brenda said. Then she looked at her subject. "Anything you would like to share, Chris?"

"I know who did it."

Twenty-four hours later, on the beach, final preparation

We are sitting on the beach in the dark. Lieutenant Ortiz reluctantly arranged to have hotel staff set up chairs in a circle and close the beach for a few hours. He is cutting me a great deal of slack; not, I think because of me, but on Sergeant Panier's recommendation.

He seems to respect her a great deal; lucky for me, I suppose.

Everyone should be here shortly and we can begin.

Everyone's angry at me except Tony and those two nautical monster slayers. No one here knows who the killer is but Courtney has agreed to help with the denouement.

Marie doesn't care much; maybe she's hoping to beat up another guy.

Tony whisked me away from the crowd today, to feed me Margaritas in the deck bar. I'm going to have to remember what a good friend he's been.

Kate's furious and hasn't spoken to me all day, except to remind me that I'm being a fucking asshole.

"You need this drama; you fucking over the hill *never-was* detective. Tell the police what you know and then we get on that plane tomorrow and get off this island. Or do you love being the one with a big secret?"

"No, I don't Kate; I know a big one about you and I have never told a soul."

"That's a low blow. You would hold that over me?"

"No dammit, I just want you to understand that I know when to talk, when to shut my fucking mouth, and when to hold on for the right moment."

"Well aren't you fucking omnipotent in your wisdom."

That's how it was. Even Brenda, who rarely lets this kind of thing show, is cool to me today.

And Roxy is incandescent with anger; I guess she's the only one I told.

Roxy and Chris, by telephone

"No way, dad. No fucking way! This is crazy." Her voice started loud but quickly quieted. I could picture her looking around the station at curious colleagues.

"I know what I'm doing." Her gasp was audible.

"Dad, I get that I grew up with nutty shrinks but I am the fucking cop here! Her voice temporarily raised again. Then it lowered dramatically. "You can't ask me to sit on this information."

"This will work, Roxy. If it isn't over tonight, tell whoever you want. You're the cop..."

"Gee thanks."

"But as far as I can see there's no proof. The second killer will walk away and never be seen again." We paused, at a temporary impasse. Roxy had the fiery temperament, but I never would have been able to manipulate her sister like this.

I was far less confident than I sounded but I couldn't let her hear it in my voice.

"You have the picture?" I said.

"Yeah, it came through on my cell."

"Okay, check it out. Can you phone me back by five?"

"Oh sure, no worries, wouldn't want you confronting a merciless killer without the information you need. You're sure about this?"

"It came out through hypnosis."

"Oh Christ. Fine, this is your last bloody hurrah. And if anything happens to you or mom, I swear I'll kill you myself."

"That's my girl."

Ten minutes with Courtney

I found her on the beach, sitting beside Marie, and kneeled beside her.

"I need to talk to you and Miles," I said.

"Not me?" Marie said with a wink. Courtney jumped in.

"He's just ahead on the beach, let's go."

Moments later, Courtney and I were standing, back to the beach, as if chatting with each other while gazing at the ocean.

"Tell Miles…"

"You can tell him…"

"Miles, I have a couple of questions for you. I know who the killer is."

"He says, 'Dammit Allard, tell the police'."

"There's almost no proof but I think we can take advantage of our situation and get some."

"Sounds like more of your bullshit, Allard. What's your plan?"

I told him.

"Could work," he admitted. "I'm not sure I can do what you're asking."

"I can do it." I turned towards Courtney, confused.

"Sorry?"

"Lucy's here too, she's been a ghost for 200 years, she's angry, and says together with Miles, we can make this happen."

I glanced over to where I thought Miles stood.

"A bit to the right, Chris."

"Well," I said to Miles. "You in?"

Courtney adopted her gruff voice: "Don't fuck it up, Allard."

In the bar with Tony, over Margaritas

"You looking forward to going home tomorrow?" I asked Tony. The mid afternoon sun was just beginning its long descent. With Brenda off having a nap, Tony had produced a large black cigar.

"I think he used less tequila in this one," Tony said, "I told him to use lots of Tequila because my friend Chris is *loco* and needs calming down."

He pulled a lighter from his pocket and began to incinerate the tip of the cigar. For him, smoking and drinking were serious business.

"He must have been troubled by your request." Tony nodded, looking again at the drink. "Are you going to answer my question?"

"Yes, but I have to say that in its way, this has been the best fucking vacation in years. Not boring."

"No," I said, "not boring." We sat for a moment. He blew a cloud of smoke between us.

I loved the smell of cigars though I would never admit that around Kate. Playing the "I'm sick with cholera" card, she had avoided seeing one between my lips the entire vacation.

"We going to catch a killer tonight?" He asked.

"I hope so."

"Are you scared?"

"Yeah, a little." He took another contemplative puff.

"I had to face down an 800 pound Sasquatch once, unarmed and sober," he said.

Oh God, here we go.

"Yeah, heard this before; and Colin Kowlchuk was up a tree with a rifle trained on the escaped monkey, or whatever it was."

He smiled. He was still wearing that stupid ball cap and smiling through the dark shadows of his unshaved beard, still mostly black while his hair was white.

"I asked Colin about that once, you know. He denied it. He said that your trip to Sioux consisted of you and him sitting around drinking in his garage."

"We swore to keep it secret."

"Uh huh." My phone rang. We both looked down at the table. I picked it up.

Five minutes later when I hung up Tony was looking at me intently. He had even put the cigar down.

"I didn't hear the details," he said, "but when Roxy is yelling at you she sounds like my daughter, Ashley." I didn't answer. "So, Chris, were you right?"

"Yeah, I was." I paused. For a moment I thought I was going to shed a tear.

"I've got another cigar," Tony said. "You want it?"

The sun hovered over the horizon in a warm bath of orange light.

"Yes, I do. And let's get another round."

The final challenge

Kate, me, Tony and Brenda arrived first, around 9 pm. The alcohol had worn off and I felt my nerves quivering in anticipation. I could still taste the tannic astringency of the tobacco in my throat.

The air felt heavy with ozone, heat lightening flashed in the distance.

Tony planted a bottle of rum in the sand beside his chair.

I was realizing what a fool I would look if this party went south. There was much that could go wrong.

Courtney and Marie were next, ushered to their seats by an unsmiling member of the hotel staff, dressed, incongruously, in a white waistcoat. Courtney glanced at me and delivered a small smile; an act that did not escape Kate's notice.

Finally the police – Canadian and Dominican – arrived in a bloc. Once seated in a circle, England, Piper, Zhang, sat together beside Panier and Ortiz. The latter barked an order in Spanish at the waiter who immediately turned and left. The Dominican detective turned to me.

"Mister Allard," he began, "You have been a strange and constant figure in this series of crimes. Several times I have been tempted to escort you, your wife and friends to the first plane leaving for Canada.

"And yet, you have an odd history of solving murders in Canada, and my colleague, Sergeant Panier, insists that you are an asset to this investigation. I trust her very much and therefore you remain."

I was listening to his words but also his tone. My plan involved something very much like group hypnosis, and it would need to be pitch perfect in its execution.

Like any good family therapist, I watched everyone in the circle at the same time. Ortiz, with a strong melodious voice was doing my job for me, along with the wind swishing through the palm fronds and the splashing of the waves.

A small lamp had been positioned in the middle of the circle, providing something of a campfire effect.

"So Mister Allard, you have one crack at this. Everyone is together. You say you have something important to tell us. Go ahead please."

All eyes turned towards me. I had expected Kate to be radiating her usual skepticism, but I could tell she was more worried, even terrified, of what might happen.

"Thank you, Lieutenant. I appreciate the faith you are putting me. I understand that this is an unusual circumstance. I will need you all to bear with me while I provide some context.

"Some of us here knew an athletic gruff voiced cop, striding through Sioux Lookout; handsome like the Marborough Man, twenty years ago. So last year when we saw a skinny bearded tourist smelling of liquor, it never occurred to us that it might be Doug Miles.

"Most of you are aware that in the wake of grieving his wife, Miles accepted a job as an undercover officer, playing a corrupt alcoholic version of himself. He excelled at this job, though like many undercover assignments, it came at a cost.

"He confused his son, alienated his friends and humiliated himself in front of colleagues."

I called up reserves from my core, lungs and stomach. With hypnosis you can use different voices; "sing song", and monotone being the most common. A strong even monotone was the right call for these circumstances.

"Miles had only just begun making contact with some underworld figures when he decided to take a break and go on a vacation; as a sidebar he would search out and identify two associates of the money laundering racket. Word was they were on vacation here, though obviously under an alias.

"Unfortunately, they identified him first. Miles cover was burned. Someone, somewhere, knew he was still working for the OPP and leaked it to cartel assassins.

"This was one undercover cop who could be easily disposed of; apparently hitting his head on an empty beach in the night while drunk, falling in the water and drowning.

"One of these criminals was Alex Ventura; big, strong and lethal. He is neutralized now but I'm guessing he's not disclosed much in custody." I glanced at Ortiz who shook his head.

"So who was this companion? And who would Ventura travel with?"

I saw something on the beach yesterday; a scorch mark on a thigh. We knew someone had a cell phone short out in their pocket during the rape and murder of Sabrina Maxwell, and I don't think it was Ventura…"

Again, I looked at Ortiz and again he shook his head.

"So last night Brenda Price hypnotized me in front of my friends, and regressed me back to our trip last year, where I wandered around the beach, the hotel and grounds of the resort until I found Alex Ventura.

"The day after we found Mile's body, Kate and I were down for breakfast and seated across from another couple; Molly and Steve; who sounded like any other dumb Canadian couple, making enquiries about the excitement on the beach.

"It was brief unmemorable encounter but I used the trance state to take a good look at his companion."

I was subtly lowering my voice; all I would need is light trance… an uncomfortable ripple passed through the group. Everyone was listening.

"I really didn't get a good look at Molly; she was dolled up in a floppy hat, huge sunglasses and a shapeless beach robe. But of course, that makes sense; in a place like this, a white heterosexual couple from Canada is just background noise. Most of us fit into that category.

"So yesterday, I saw "Molly" on the beach, along with the scorch mark. I was triggered then, but after the hypnosis I was all but certain.

"Who would know that Miles was undercover? The obvious answer is someone on the inside. A leak in the OPP; a man or woman who learned that Doug Miles was on to them."

Eyes were moving now, but I had to keep the attention on me.

"That job should have been easy and ruled an accident, but Miles was found by a group of nosy tourists who knew him. This was the true coincidence from the point of view of the killers.

"And worse; one of those tourists, started asking question about his death; here and in Canada. And then they decided to come back to the Dominican Republic.

"So Molly and Steve came back themselves to check out and, if required, eliminate the threat.

"First they tried the easy way; delivering water laced with cholera baccilli to Kate and I. Unfortunately for them I chose that morning to stick to a boozy breakfast and only Kate got sick.

"So now they had to do it the hard way; plant a bomb and get out of the country. Molly could disappear into a hoodie more easily than Steve so she planted the C4 on the boat.

"But she was noticed by an inquisitive teenager as she disembarked.

"She also hadn't counted on a brave and resourceful naval officer being onboard. So we survived the bomb and the threat shifted onto a cocky and naive 16 year old from Napanee named Sabrina Maxwell.

"They killed her together, but Molly had received a call and had to leave the next day, which left Ventura at loose ends; establishing a cover story of his wife leaving him.

"Like most sociopaths, he was glib, impulsive and sexually voracious. The rape of Sabrina was gratuitous, and seducing Courtney Snow was the act of an amoral hobbyist."

I could see Courtney stiffen. Everyone was getting uncomfortable but hanging on my words.

"When the killer learned of Courtney in the form of a discarded brassiere; her descent into madness accelerated, and continues now; it has to; even assuming a degree of sociopathy, this has been much too much; failing, failing failing… *fucking up* every attempt to make this problem go away."

My main moment was getting closer.

"She was already on the brink of mania, and only just appearing otherwise; she changed her appearance for yet another role but…"

Time to move in for the kill.

"I spoke today to Detective Roxane Kosinski – my daughter – of the OPP. I also sent her a photograph, which she has now identified.

"Morgan Fleur, born in Argentina, immigrant to Canada, and resident of Montreal, and associate of criminals, fell off the map five years ago according to the Sûreté du Québec. I have a picture of her, a little dated, on my cell phone for the police."

The tension had continued to escalate. Most had guessed; I noticed Zhang and Ortiz shifting their posture.

"Sergeant Piper," I said in as conversational a tone as I could could muster, "Did Gwen fly down here with you and Inspector Zhang?"

"No, she was already here…" His voice trailed off, and he looked to his side. He was last to get it. I was looking at her too. Yes, now I could see the madness. I made eye contact.

"Morgan, I'm betting Courtney's bra pushed you over the edge. Raping Sabrina; all in a day's work, but knowing Courtney had the chance to *baise ton copain*."

ME ESTOY RIENDO DE TI!

Miles had spent the day fucking with the radio in the bar. By the end of the afternoon the barman was drinking rum straight out of the bottle, but Miles had mastered the task and his cue.

The high pitched blast from the radio ran through our group like a jolt of lightening. Kate grabbed my arm and even Courtney and I, who knew it was coming, were shocked.

We all turned our heads towards the sound and when we turned back, someone new had arrived.

She stood in the centre of the circle, *black, beautiful, spectral and terrible.* She glowed and fire raged in her eyes. She pointed an accusing finger at Gwen England and said:

"YOU killed her!"

And that's when my plan went off the rails.

Kate

This was over the top, even for Chris. He's just lucky no one there had a bad heart. The tension was unbearable.

But who was that woman? She was suddenly there in the middle of the circle, then gone, just like that.

Everyone was looking at Gwen; three of the cops, Ortiz, Panier and Zhang were easing their right hands towards their belts; Marie and Tony's hands were tightening into fists.

And Gwen; Chris said she was mad, and she looked it. But when she moved, she moved so fast that no one reacted in time.

She was on her feet, roughly clutching Brenda by the shirt collar, holding a small silver pistol to her head. Her first words were directed at Chris:

"You fucking…" She paused, *"You fucking piece of shit… I should put a bullet in you right now…"* Her face, once attractive, was a mask of hate and rage. I had never seen anyone that angry at Chris, including me; which was saying a lot.

She jerked Brenda closer. Brenda looked over at her husband. It was a strange, almost happy, look. But Gwen wasn't done:

"I have car waiting and a boat to catch." She waved the gun round the circle, "Grandma here is coming with me." She pulled Brenda to her feet. She shook some black hair away from her face.

"If anyone leaves their seat before I am in the car, she gets a bullet in the head; *EVERYBODY GOT THAT!*

No one spoke for a moment until Tony; ice cold, eye's hooded and narrowed to slits spoke: "Don't kill her. We need her."

"I don't give a fuck what you need," Gwen started, but Tony interrupted.

"Not talking to you, you fucking bitch."

Gwen started to back away, dragging Brenda along with her. As she disappeared into the dark; no one spoke, everyone listened. Guns appeared and finally Ortiz started to speak rapidly in Spanish to Panier.

But one more shock awaited. Moments after we lost sight of them, we heard a hideous shiek; more than one; two voices. One, screaming in anger; one screaming in pain.

It was over in seconds; everyone was on their feet when the sounds stopped abruptly, then yet another woman appeared from the dark.

She was young, maybe twenty, beautiful, red hair flying in the ocean wind, and topless. All the men's eyes widened, except Tony who just shook his head and smiled.

And mad? This one was mad as a hatter; you could see it in her eyes. This was one crazy unhinged bitch. She halted just outside the circle, glancing first at Tony.

"*She'll live*," she said, dismissively, regretfully. Then she approached Chris.

"*You left me alone, heartbroken, in the cold*." She then glared at me with hate in her eyes. She was every bit as scary as Morgan/Gwen.

"You should leave," Tony said. And with that simple command, she turned and started running towards the balustrade; fast, faster than a woman should be able to run.

We were left in silence. Until we heard a woman – Morgan - groan, up the beach, where she lay bleeding in the sand.

Chris leaned over, embraced me and started to shake.

Prior to take off

The day began with Dr. Fernando making one last trip to our room; this time he was here to see me.

"You doing better, dude?" he said, in his very un-Dominican accent.

"Yeah, whatever you gave me last night did the job. Bit shaky, but I slept well, ready to go home.

"Awesome."

"How's the other lady?" I asked. Kate glared at me.

"She'll live," he said flatly. Then he returned to his usual affable self and gave both of us a quick check.

"Cleared for take off," he said finally, chuckling at his own joke.

After thanking him for all his help, we went down to find our friends in the buffet.

Tony was working on his third Mimosa and Brenda was sipping coffee; looking wan, and older than ever.

"Rough night?" I said.

"Don't be such an asshole, Chris!" Kate said. "Brenda could have been killed."

"You should see the other guy," Tony said. This elicited a chuckle from Brenda.

"You social workers are fucking nuts," Kate said with feeling. She looked at Brenda. "When we called Tony said you just went back to your room and went to bed. We didn't see you at all."

"Yeah, I was scared, I kind of snuck back."

"Did you see that crazy girl?" Kate asked.

Brenda didn't look up. "I heard her."

"They didn't find her." Brenda was being evasive but Kate was trying to make sense of the events.

"I don't think they will," I said. Brenda looked up at me. But Tony raised his Mimosa.

"Well, the fucking social work detective strikes again; more killers taken off the books by Mister Chris fucking Allard."

At this point, Kate theatrically sighed, shrugged and lifted a glass with the rest of us.

"Does this mean its over?" I said.

"I think so," Tony replied. "Sergeant Panier wants to meet with Brenda before the bus leaves for the airport but otherwise, everything's clear. I think Zhang and Piper are staying for another couple of days to clear things up.

"I don't know if they will extradite Morgan but either way, she's going to be out of the loop for a while." We all shuddered. The waiter arrived with a tray of Mimosas.

Kate made a show of pushing her water glass aside and taking a deep sip of her drink.

"Well," she said, "on the plus side, Chris has seen more fresh new tits on this trip than ever before."

Brenda giggled, then she began to laugh, then laugh too much, before sucking in her breath as a few tears leaked from the corner of her eyes. We were starting to worry but she held up a hand.

"That's funny," she said. Tony grinned.

Courtney

I can't believe Marie's thrown me out of the room again.

And last night; fuck! How embarrassing; my blue bra drove psycho chick over the edge! After it was over all Marie could talk about was what a fun vacation it had been. Sex! Violence! Mayhem!

At one point she stopped babbling and said, "Courtney, do you think I am some kind of a sociopath, for liking this so much?"

"Yes Marie, God yes; have you not being listening?"

"Okay, so you won't be mad if I find one more guy to fuck tomorrow morning. Aren't you horny?"

I was not, but it was another lovely day in paradise and I was walking the beach while she did Lord knows what with a German guy she found who could speak a few words of French.

I found Miles and Lucy staring out at the sea.

"It's time for me to go," Miles said. "I can see the light. My wife is there." He turned to me: "Tell Allard… *thanks*, tell him… tell him I'm glad there was a social worker from Scarborough on this case."

He turned to Lucy and smiled. "You are wonderful, you were so brave last night. I'll tell your mother that you will be right up." And he was gone. I turned to Lucy.

"Aren't you going with him?"

"No, I have one more person to talk to before I leave."

"You were amazing last night," I said. She smiled shyly.

"Thank you Courtney for everything. I felt something last night I never felt before, in life or death."

"What?"

"*Powerful.*"

She smiled again, less shyly. "That is something I will remember for eternity."

We said our goodbyes and I turned and walked away. I met Sergeant Panier at the foot of the stairway.

"She's waiting for you," I said. Then, "May I hug you?" She wrapped her arms around me.

Sergeant Evangeline Panier

"On behalf on the government of the República Dominicana and the government of Canada I wish to thank you for service to our respective countries in aiding in the capture of two dangerous killers."

Why not - in this strange case - offer the government's gratitude to a ghost? After all, she was a brave witness who, at great effort, revealed herself to a heinous killer.

I believe Ortiz is going to take a short break after this case; spend time with his wife and kids. He could use it; he is a good man; better than most. I think he recognized a fellow spirit in this Sergeant Miles, though the two never met.

So Lucy Jones, filled with beauty and pride, bowed low, wished me well and disappeared into the light.

The Canadians seem full of surprises. I certainly never expected to meet another medium here of all places. And Chris Allard; he is…annoying, but he came through and made all the proper deductions.

But the biggest surprise; well, I am meeting with her now.

Brenda

I had no idea what this meeting was about and to be truthful, I felt like I had the biggest hangover in history.

It was not so much remorse I felt; *she* – the other Brenda - didn't feel any, and only emerged in a dire emergency. No, it was the same as always; the exhilaration, the violence, strength and speed.

Afterward, in the room, I begged Tony to fuck me; I wanted him so badly… but he refused; I was getting younger when I turned – this time only 20ish – and he wouldn't do it while I was not in my right mind. Besides, he said old Brenda had really upped her game; he was willing to wait.

Old Brenda; ugh. I was already looking ten years older than I was. Tony had cheated – often – when we were young, but that had stopped a long time ago. He would never leave me; no matter what happened.

He loves me and is proud of the woman I am…

"Mrs. Price?" Sergeant Panier was standing on the beach. She had just turned away from the water. Was that a tear in her eye? She noticed me noticing, and shook it away. "May we walk together?" she said.

We slowly made our way along the water's edge. Today brown Pelicans were dive bombing the water, just beyond the guard line. A school of fish?

Panier began to talk in a conversational tone.

"When I was a child in Haiti my mother became a Christian. Her mother was a vodou Mambo – do you know what that is?

"Yes." Uh oh, where was this going?

"My mother meant well; I am a Christian too, but my grandmother told me many stories, and passed on a few understandings… and a few jars… before she died."

Panier stopped and picked up a flat rock. She threw it sideways into the water. It skipped three times before hitting a wave. She seemed to be associating into her girlhood.

"I became a police officer but often return home. My country has had many challenges; the aftermath of the earthquake was perhaps the worst one in recent times, and my family is there.

"A few years ago, I was home with my mother, when a series of murders broke out in the slums of Port au Prince. What made these stand out were the savagery, and indications that they were committed a young white man.

"The killings ended as abruptly as they began and coincided with the disappearance of an older man; a white Canadian doctor…"

"Dr. Jack Ells," I said. Panier looked up.

"Yes, Dr. Jack Ells."

We both looked up as one of the Pelicans skimmed the water, narrowly avoiding a swimmer. "To continue my story, I knew a man named Honore – an acolyte of my grandmother; he worked at Dr. Ells' clinic.

"I met him one day and out of the memory and respect for my grandmother, he confirmed the question I put to him.

"There is a certain herb, thought extinct." She shrugged, suggesting an opinion contrary to popular thought. "This herb now only exists in a few hidden places, under supervision, though a supply was thought to have fallen into the wrong hands…

"It is deeply corrupting to the taker; few can handle its effects; Ells could not… Mrs Price, how did it get into you?"

"Champagne," I said, "Ells sent over champagne. My friend, Tony and I all drank it." I was now reminiscing, though also putting myself at risk. I liked this Panier but…

"And how did it effect them?"

"My friend is like me. Tony is immune." Panier looked up.

"Your husband is an unusual man."

"Don't get me started." She shrugged again, and laughed lightly.

"I will never call Canadians dull again." We continued to walk until we reached the far side of the beach. Standing by a rock face, she continued.

"And Ells?"

"No one will be seeing him again. His alter ego fell off a roof."

"I see."

She seemed to be thinking within herself. "Mrs Price, you do not seem to be someone who takes too much credit for herself."

"I don't need it."

"Nevertheless, I find myself today offering gratitude to those who may not normally receive it. It seems an older woman social worker from Canada has rid my country of not one but several scourges."

Then: "Do you drink tea?"

What was this about; were we going for tea?

"Sometimes."

"I want to send a package of tea to your home in Canada. Two of the tea bags will be marked a little different than the others; one for your friend and the other for you."

"Something special about this tea?"

"You may not choose to drink it, but if you do you will lose the ability to transition and regain the youth appropriate to your age. *C'est tout?*"

She ended the conversation abruptly. I had a feeling she was as uncomfortable with softer emotions as I was.

"Thank you," I said simply. "My friend and I will thank you for your gift, and probably Tony too."

She laughed. The moment had changed. She lifted her right hand towards the distant stairway: *"Allons?"*

July 2020, a deck in Kingston, Ontario

"Holy shit, Brenda, you look like a million bucks. You been working out?"

She laughed loudly; a witchy uncharacteristicly rich laugh for her.

"Yeah, that must be it, Chris."

"And did you…" Tony jumped in:

"One word about hair dye and you are so fucked, bro."

"Chris!" Kate said. She wanted to glare but the jolly mood was infectious; we were all laughing.

Rain threatened earlier but the clouds shifted mid-afternoon, leaving a warm dim sun to sink gracefully into the west.

We were catching up, talking about our kids; Kate and me bragging about our grandson, and it turns out, the glowing and beautiful Brenda breaking the news about their son Kyle's partner recently discovered pregnancy. Hence the champagne.

"Who the fuck thought I would ever be a Grampa?" Tony said.

"You'll be awesome," Kate said.

"Hey, Chris, you'll never guess who I ran into at Lemoine Point." Tony, perhaps spurred on by Brenda, had been on a fitness kick of late and haunting the beautiful trails of a nearby park. I guessed what was coming.

"I found Courtney talking to her boyfriend, Nick. I didn't see him but she introduced me. He said to say "Hi" to the infamous Chris. And she did too."

Kate's eyes narrowed and she provided me with a firm bop to the thigh for good measure.

"What are they up to?"

"She and Marie are off to the arctic for something - no idea what - radioactive giant Walrus? Who the fuck knows?"

"Do you have any news for us?" Brenda asked. She winked at Kate, who was happy to divert the topic away from buxom ichthyologists who said hi to her husband.

"Roxanne has been able to share a few things with us," Kate said, stopping for another sip of champagne. "Apparently the Dominican government isn't giving up Alex Ventura or Morgan Fleur any time soon."

"Can you blame them?" I said. Kate glanced over but kept going.

"I don't know how hard they're trying; there's no extradition treaty and as much as they want the killer of one of their own here, both *are* being punished. And if Morgan Fleur came home there might be some embarrassing revelations as to how a known criminal became an OPP translator.

"They can rot," Brenda said. This wasn't a very social worky thing to say but we knew that Brenda still drove to Napanee to visit Sabrina's mother. Carrie Maxwell's wounds would never completely heal.

We took a moment to contemplate that. We heard the rolling cadence of distant thunder, and a quick breeze through the apple leaves. The storm was coming back.

"Did anyone ever hear again from Ortiz and Panier?" I said.

"Sergeant Panier sent Brenda some nice herbal tea," Tony said, a strange smile flitting across his face. "A kind of Haitian tonic. She said that all was well and she and Ortiz were hard at work."

"Whatever was in that tonic, it sure worked, Brenda, I can't get over how good you look."

"You said that already, Chris," Kate growled, "let it go." She rapped my thigh again.

"Well, at least nobody managed to kill, Chris," Tony said cheerfully. Kate and Brenda looked at each other in theatrical silence. Tony tried again:

"So where do you want to go next year?"

"After everything that happened this year, illness, murder, bombs, mayhem… you still want to go on vacation…" Kate's voice trailed off before perking up again: "I'm in."

"Me too," said Brenda.

"Fuck ya!" Tony said.

"Well that's it then," I said. "Let's make some plans."

Thunder continued to rumble in the distance but we had another drink before the rain forced us in.

The End

www.ingramcontent.com/pod-product-compliance
Lightning Source LLC
Chambersburg PA
CBHW021142130626
46554CB00005B/1624